SIRIARNA

PRUDENCE WILLETT

SIRIARNA

DIVINE DESTINIES BOOK 1

A catalogue record for this book is available from the National Library of Australia.
ISBN: 978-0-6456992-2-7 (ebook)
ISBN: 978-0-6456992-3-4 (paperback)

Cover designed by MiblArt
Map created by Lawson Willett
Chapter art designed by Abigail Jane Wilkins

For those of you who love a fantasy story;

With power, adventure and mythological glory;

A romantic subplot weaves its way through;

And is expressed from multiple point of views;

Unravel twists, unfold suspense;

Enjoy your journey, with love Prudence.

PRONUNCIATION & REALM GUIDE

CHARACTERS:

Siriarna	–	Si-ree-ah-nah
Alexandraya	–	Alex-an-dray-ah
Roman	–	Row-man
Braxton	–	Brax-ton
Melodie	–	Mel-o-dee
Davina	–	Dav-ee-nah
Simeon	–	Sim-ee-on
Eloise	–	Elle-o-eez
High Power		
Omnisensus	–	Om-nee-sen-sus

GODS:

Zeus	–	Zoos
Eileithyia	–	Ee-lee-th-ee-ah
Eleos	–	El-ee-os
Psyche	–	Sy-kee
Apollo	–	A-pol-lo
Hermes	–	Her-meez
Hera	–	Heh-rah

REALMS:

Sky Realm	–	Mount Olympus
Progression Realm	–	Evolirium (Ev-o-leer-i-um)
Surface Realm	–	Earth
Home Realm	–	Semi God dwelling
Working Realm	–	The Between

Evolirium
Mountains
Dormitory Huts
Meadows
Ovallium Forest
Grassy Mounds
Dock
Zen
River
Light Pillars
Zeneym Arena
Electrical Boards
Sports Fields
Learning Facility
Void

CHAPTER 1

Siriarna

I was gifted with the ability to remember every word I read. And I hated that 'so-called' gift.

My guide parents, Linus and Stefanie, are constantly bragging about my photographic memory to everyone; usually at one of their elaborate masquerade parties. Like, they are nauseatingly proud. It's embarrassing. Especially the way they parade me around in front of their guests, showing me off as this highly skilled semi god—which I'm anything but. The anonymity of the mask is my saving grace at these parties. It provides a shield, a sequined haven where I can fantasise about being someone else, a person who is in control of their magic. It's how I manage to endure these events.

But the reality is, I dream about being like all the other semi gods here in the Home Realm, *normal*. Every night I wish to the Fates that I wake up and my fledgling powers cooperate. But my pleas remain unheard, and my magic remains sketchy.

Am I really the offspring of both god and mortal?

With the festive season ending and the parties finally drawing to a close, I have time to prepare for my relocation to the Progression Realm, and I'm spending every waking hour studying. Both guide parents chide me for continually having my nose in a book. Even though delivered affectionately, it annoys me. The books provide a sense of peace, not judgement. I know leaving them scattered messily throughout my room is cause for Stefanie's continual frustration, but I find the volumes comforting.

I am currently absorbing every written magic book available within this realm, and am making quick work of memorising the text. Surely my power will eventually follow my knowledge and settle into the smooth rhythm I see come so easily to every other semi god in the Home Realm.

Linus and Stefanie are still members of the Evolirium Alumni for high achieving students so try as they might, they can never truly understand what it's like to be magic average, or less than average in my case. They keep insisting I am fortunate to have such a great memory, that it will come in handy when studying chants and putting the spells into practice. I wish I could believe them. Right now, I'm questioning whether I even deserve a place in the Progression Realm. *Will I fit in?* I am consumed by these doubts, especially as I am leaving tomorrow.

A soft knock on my bedroom door disturbs me from my thoughts. "Can I come in?" Stefanie asks, moving the door ajar.

"Of course," I say as I force a smile.

"I wanted to have a chat with you before you leave this realm. I know how hard you have been working and how you see your gift as a curse, but honestly, Siriarna, it will come to serve you well. I believe it in my heart." Stefanie sits next to me on the floor and embraces me in a hug.

"What if my powers never evolve?" I whisper.

She reaches over and brushes the hair from my eyes. "They will. Evolirium is built to harness each semi god's talent. You'll see. You need to trust the process. You'll be so happy there, just like I was."

That was the last piece of advice Stefanie imparted before the chariot arrived, ready to escort me to Evolirium and to my new life.

Ready or not, here I come.

*****

Upon realm arrival, I am chaperoned directly to the Learning Facility to meet with High Power Omnisensus, the Director of Students and Realm Master. His greeting is warm and friendly. I like him on sight. He ushers me into his office, where another student is already seated in one of the two leather chairs opposite his desk. Running his hands through his unruly salt and pepper shaded hair, he says, "Siriarna, please meet Alexandraya. I have selected her to help you settle in. Is that okay with you Alexandraya?" he asks with such joviality, it's more a courtesy than a request.

"Of course, Sir," she replies. But the way she is eyeballing me indicates that is not the case.

"Wonderful. Siriarna, we are very glad to have you here. You two may leave," he says already distracted by one of the buzzing orbs on his desk.

Leaving the Authority's office, I turn to Alexandraya, "How long have you been living on Evolirium?"

"I arrived when I was twelve. My guide parents recognised my talent early and knew how crucial getting a start on my magic would be. These four years have been invaluable. Why have you been so delayed? Sixteen is just sad. You'll never get your skills up to speed before Propensity Selections in two years. You might as well return to the Home Realm now. I really don't have time to waste on a hopeless case. You're just too 'basic'."

Swallowing the emerging lump in my throat, I reply, "My guide parents wanted to wait until they felt it was the right time." I try to keep my voice neutral while defending my late realm arrival, but I hear it start to crack and the pitch begin to rise.

She rolls her eyes and huffs, "Whatever."

"Where to first?" I ask brushing off the previous insult while trying to keep up with her long strides.

"I'm going to the Zen to meet my friends. I don't care where you go, as long as it's nowhere near me." With a flick of her long jet-black hair, she disappears through the Learning Facility's double entrance doors leaving them swinging in my face.

Rather than follow behind her, I turn and retreat down the seemingly endless hallway. Wandering left at the first junction, I find myself outside the Knowledge Room and breathe a long sigh of relief.

Now this is what I'm talking about.

Entering the enormous space, I am instantly hit with the woody, slightly vanilla scent of thousands of books. I draw in a deep breath, then release it from my lungs, and the tension leaves my body. I am greeted by dozens of rows of shelves lining the walls, circling to the centre of the room in a crescent shape. I can't help but trail my fingers across the books; there are just so many of them. A small staircase is hidden by bookshelves at the centre of the library. Curiosity sparked I descend, excited to see what lies beneath. A visual haven appears before me and gratitude fills my heart. I immediately flop onto one of the plush couches surrounding the perimeter of the room and grab a pillow to hug. The space is amazing and I'm the only one here. *How can such a treasure be empty?*

"There you are. I've wasted my whole afternoon trying to find you." Alexandraya spits as she reaches the bottom of the Reading Hub.

"I'm sorry, I lost track of time."

"The Authority wants me to show you to our accommodations. Let's go."

I grab my satchel, and jump to my feet. Alexandraya's scowl and impatience leaves me twitching.

We walk through a grassy arena, but I barely have time to take in the surroundings. Alexandraya is on a mission, and it seems she plans on fulfilling her obligations as quickly as she can to be free from her new burden—me.

Approaching the dormitories, I am taken aback by the fact that they are individual huts. Minus Alexandraya, things on Evolirium are looking up.

"Over there, past these huts, to the left and round the corner is your hut. Your belongings will be outside the front door." She pivots on her heel and vanishes, leaving me to find my own way.

Following her rushed directions, I walk around the interconnecting pathways until I stumble across my belongings. They are positioned outside a neat looking hut at the end of a row of mirrored dorms. *Perfect.*

A voice from behind startles me. "Can I help you with those?"

Turning, I settle my gaze on a guy with short cropped

sandy hair.

"I'm Roman, it's a pleasure to live in your lane."

A laugh escapes my lips. "Sure, grab a bag."

CHAPTER 2

Siriarna

Stefanie was wrong! My magic has not progressed.

It's been two years since I arrived at Evolirium, and I skip power progression classes wherever possible. It's how I ended up in the Authority's office today. I remember sitting here on my arrival when I was paired with Alexandraya. What a disaster that turned out to be. Her torment remains consistent and so has our mutual dislike. I had such hope for this year, but it is proving to be the same as the previous—magic useless.

My thoughts are dragged back to the present. "Are you listening to me Siriarna?" the exasperated Authority announces.

It was only a matter of time before I was caught. The Authority clears his throat, waiting for an answer.

"Yes, High Power Omnisensus," I reply vaguely.

This response affords me another half an hour of lectures. I guess I deserve it.

I make a pledge to try my best to focus and attend all remaining physical sessions before selections. *This time, I really mean it.*

After my release, I rush into the corridor and almost knock the books straight from Alexandraya's arms.

"Watch it 'basic'. Gods, you are still so useless. You really don't belong in this realm. I'm surprised you're still here. Surely you realise you won't be anointed at the Propensity Selections. Your powers are just so, well, 'basic'." She throws back her head and laughs at her own joke.

"Sorry, I didn't see you." I reply meekly.

"Well, how could you with all that hair covering your eyes." She spews the words whilst continuing on her way without a backward glance.

Whilst I'm used to Alexandraya's insults, I do fear she is right. At this rate I won't qualify for a Propensity, and I will be forced to make a decision about where my remaining 500-year future lies. I silently curse my stubborn magic. It only seems to cooperate when moving electrical currents—a small and insignificant portion of the 6th Propensity. Damn the Fates for continually ignoring my desperate pleas for flowing magic.

Hear me this time, please hear me.

Brushing off Alexandraya's insult, I continue down the hallway and head straight back to the Knowledge Room, my safe place. However, her insult is lodged firmly in the back of my mind. To distract myself from sinking further into dark thoughts, I immerse myself in a new book, losing track of time until the shrill sounding class bell jolts me back to the present. Dropping the book and grabbing my satchel, I sprint from the library. I don't want to be late to class again and end up back in High Power Omnisensus' office. Especially, so soon after promising to attend physical lessons.

As I open the classroom door sweaty and flustered, I notice the room is already full. I am the last to arrive, as usual. I lower my head as 28 pairs of eyes turn to stare at me. Melodie reaches over and whispers to both Davina and Alexandraya. These girls have been nothing but a trio of nightmares since my arrival—I secretly call them the

TON. I've only shared the acronym with Roman. He thought it was hilarious when I first mentioned it, saying it matched their interchangeable personalities.

The only free seat left in class is right in front of the TON. I can't believe my bad luck.

"Good one 'basic'," Davina sniggers referring to my usual lateness.

I slink into my chair, bow my head forward so my hair shields my face, and I try my best to disappear.

After what feels like an eternity, the end of class bell rings and everyone evacuates in a mighty rush toward the exit. Melodie shoves an elbow into my ribs as she passes, then smiles sweetly, "Oops, sorry."

Gods I hate the TON.

Once outside, I take in a huge gulp of crisp fragrant air and count to three slowly before releasing the breath. I move through the Zeneym Arena looking for Roman.

"Hey, you made it," he says as I approach the grassy mounds under the weeping willow-bank trees.

"Barely, that last lesson was brutal."

"How so?"

"The TON."

Roman pats the ground next to him. "Tell me all about

it," he says passing me a bottle of mountain elixir.

Taking a sip of the sweet tasting refreshment, I unload the morning's events. "Well, I got caught... again. High Power Omnisensus made me promise to attend all remaining power progression classes, I was late to class, the TON made it hard to concentrate on the lesson, and my magic didn't cooperate. I think it's time to acknowledge that I am a hopeless case."

"You are not hopeless. You just need to up your practice. I'll help you. We can start tomorrow. Unless you want to join me at the light pillars now?"

He plants a quick kiss on my cheek which catches me off guard. I look to meet his gaze, but he is already standing, his tall silhouette towering above me and I have to crane my neck to make eye contact. "Um, I think we should start fresh tomorrow." I say pulling out a book.

"Okay. But Siriarna, I'm serious. Tomorrow morning, no excuses."

"I said I would Roman, geez, give me *some* credit."

"Okay, okay. Walk you home after class?" he winks.

"Sure. Meet me outside the Knowledge Room?"

"As if you'd be anywhere else," he teases.

I watch him stride past the Zen River to the light

pillars. He cuts a commanding figure; the rumours circulating say he is the son of one of the Olympian Gods. I wouldn't be surprised if it was Zeus himself, even though semi gods are the result of later generations and minor deities only.

The last lesson of the day goes by without incident, and I make my way toward the Knowledge Room. Roman is already there, leaning up against the outside wall waiting for me.

"Hey, can you just wait while I swap this out?" I ask as I reach him.

"Is there anything left in there for you to read?"

"I'm sure I'll find something. I'll just be a snap."

Moments later, I am disturbed by a light tapping on my shoulder. I pivot around to find Roman looming above me with a crooked expression on his face. "It's been ages Siriarna, and you still haven't checked out a book. Let's go before it gets dark, I'm starving."

I hadn't realised I'd been browsing for so long. After I check out the book I was skimming in the stacks, I'm ready. "Righto, let's head."

Strolling through the Zen, the nickname given to the Zeneym Arena by students, past the floral meadows on our way to our dorm huts, we walk happily in comfortable silence. Giving him a sideways glance, I realise how lucky I am to have Roman as my best friend.

As he opens the door to my hut, he promptly trips over a stack of books. "My gods, you are such a slob, Siriarna."

"My space, my way."

His insult doesn't bother me in the slightest because I love the freedom of living alone. Saying that, I clear another stack of books from my couch and flop down, glad the day is over. Roman joins me after diving into my fridge and drinking my last bottle of mountain elixir in one gulp.

"Hey, I was saving that for later."

"Well, it was delicious if that's any consolation," Roman scoffs, plonking his lanky frame down next to me.

"Wanna hang out later at the Etherial Room?"

"No." I say a little too hastily. Then I add, "I'll need an early night so I can meet you at the Zen for practice tomorrow." I hate the Etherial Room and the way the in-groups swan around. It makes me feel even more awkward than usual.

Roman clutches his stomach in hysterics. "We're meeting an hour before class Siriarna, the sun will already be up. Just like you should be."

At this chastise, I throw my fluffy reading pillow straight at his head. Whilst my aim was incredibly accurate, he manages to escape contact by using the speed of light.

"Show off."

"Slob," he teases and strides out my front door singing, "See you in the morning Siriarna."

Maybe.

CHAPTER 3

Siriarna

I don't make it to the planned tutoring session with Roman. Instead, I stay in bed until the sunshine filters through my window warming my skin. Besides, how many times does one turn eighteen?

Leisurely, I step out of bed and open the wardrobe door to the mirror located on the inside. Scrutinizing my reflection, I can't see anything different. Same appearance, same feelings, same everything. I try to cast a simple image spell to lighten my very average hair colour, it's not blonde nor brunette, sitting somewhere in between. But my magic doesn't cooperate. Surprise. Not surprise. I guess my birthday wishes to the Fates were unanswered once again. It's definitely put a dampener on my celebratory spirit. I mean, I didn't expect to wake up full of confidence with magic zapping through my veins, called upon at will. Okay, I actually did. Eighteen is a big deal for a semi god. It makes the disappointment so much worse.

I dress in my white training uniform and leave the hut. No point stopping by Roman's dorm, he'll be practicing his skills at the light pillars. Surely he won't be shocked that I didn't turn up, despite my promises.

I really do want to qualify for a Propensity and I make a mental note that I will, most definitely, make the effort to rise early tomorrow morning and meet him for our intended tutoring session. After all, I am a mature eighteen year old now.

Arriving to the first lesson of the day, I spy Roman sitting in his usual spot by the window, mid row. I make my way to the vacant seat beside him and slide in, knocking the desk with a clunk.

"I see you are still as awkward as usual despite your wiser years," he says with mirth.

"Stop it, I did that on purpose to announce my arrival." I brush my bangs aside, and bat my eyelashes innocently.

"Funny. I missed you at training this morning," he rolls his eyes. "I guess I'll let you off due to it being the most auspicious of occasions. Happy Birthday by the way," he grins.

"Thanks. I feel totally different."

"You look it," he counters, softly laughing under his breath.

The lecturer enters the room and announces the day's lesson will pick up where we left off last week, discussing the Mount Olympus Council Arena and the Olympian Gods that hold voting positions.

I love studying the old textbooks and manuscripts. The images are so beautifully curated, I am drawn into the artwork, often getting lost in the nuances of brushstrokes. My fellow classmates do not hold the same passion as me and a collective groan vibrates around the room at the mention of text study. On the opposite end of the spectrum, I am delighted there is no physical skills training today. *Maybe the Fates have listened somewhat and spared me a magical embarrassment?*

*****

The last lesson flies by and Roman waits for me to pack up my satchel.

"Come on, gods you're slow," he says drumming his fingers on his work desk impatiently.

"What's the big hurry?"

"You'll see," he says cryptically.

"Argh. Okay."

I carefully place the text book in my satchel, and I'm ready to leave. Following him down the hallway, I pass the TON who are huddled together at the exit.

Why are they still here?

"Last to class, last to leave." Alexandraya says haughtily.

"Ignore her," Roman says, linking his arm through mine and steering me out the Facility's double entrance doors.

A final backward glance reveals Alexandraya following Roman with watchful eyes.

No one except Roman knows it's my birthday today. And High Power Omnisensus. The Authority called me into his office at mid break and presented me with Evolirium's signature crest lapel pin. The gold pin is shaped in a six point star, each point representing a Propensity, with an embossed "E" in its centre. It's given to students on their eighteenth birthday signifying eligibility to showcase at Propensity Selections. My birthday falls at the end of first quarter, therefore, I just scrape into this year's selections.

I was too nervous to pin it into place in front of the Authority. I pull it out now while we're walking and turn in over in my hand, admiring the way the gold sparkles in the sun, before attempting to fasten it into place. I can't help but remember Alexandraya's terse warning when we first met—that as a late realm starter, I had little chance of qualifying for a Propensity. The thought causes my eye to twitch, and I puncture my finger with the pin. "Ouch."

"Give it here," Roman says snatching the pin and expertly securing it on my training shirt collar. "There, perfect."

"What would I do without you?"

"Gods knows!"

We have reached the meadow and instead of proceeding along the pathway, Roman leads me into the field.

"Hey, where are we going?" I say puzzled. "I thought

we were going to hang out at yours?"

"Small detour," he says with a cheeky glint in his pale blue eyes.

Roman takes my hand and starts running toward the little rock cluster we call 'our spot', dragging me with him.

My breath catches in my throat as a dining al fresco comes into view. As we get closer, I see dozens of tiny candles dotted throughout the rocks and a luxurious feathery blanket positioned on the ground in front. A jug of spiced elixir is sitting on a tray surrounded by tiny spherical delicacies dipped in chocolate and flecked with gold dust.

"Well, what do you think?" Roman asks.

"It's perfect," my voice croaks, and I bow my head as I lower myself onto the blanket, attempting to conceal the well of emotion building up inside.

Once seated, Roman expertly casts a spell and the candles flicker to light.

"Show off," I chastise through choked back sobs of delight.

"Friends First Always," he says grinning while pouring me a glass of elixir. "Cheers."

"Cheers." I repeat, delighted by this afternoon's

surprise.

The last rays of sunlight disappear behind the realm and the soft glowing beams from the rising moon shimmer across the meadow. In response to the reflected light cast, moonflowers and evening primrose burst into flower. Roman's flickering candles add to the ambiance, creating a flawless backdrop.

"Close your eyes and hold out your hand."

I giggle but do as I'm asked. A cool object is pressed into my palm.

"Open your eyes."

In my hand is a glass bookmark with multiple strands of light suspended within it. Varying shades of purple from lilac to aubergine are dancing between the transparent layers, made more brilliant when they catch the reflection of the moonlight.

"Happy Birthday, Siriarna."

"It's so beautiful, I absolutely love it." I whisper, turning the bookmark over and letting the colours swirl before my eyes. It really is the most thoughtful gift I've ever received. "How did you make it?" I ask in awe.

"Magic," he winks.

CHAPTER 4

Siriarna

Bright and early, I manage to drag myself out of bed and dress in my white training uniform before heading to the Zeneym Arena to meet Roman. I can't let him down again today, especially after yesterday's brilliant birthday surprise.

My body protests the earlier rise time, but I push on through persistent yawns. Tying my hair back and straightening my bangs, I hear the hut door groan in sympathy as it closes behind me.

When I reach the Zen, it is already a hive of activity. Students are making the most of practising their skills with only seven days remaining until Propensity

Selections. A line has formed around the light pillars, and this is where I find Roman, waiting to practice his favourite skill. He is surrounded by the TON, and Alexandraya has her hand on his shoulder. He glances up, spots me, and raises his hand in a wave. He holds up 5 fingers indicating he'll be with me soon. To his side, looking in my direction, Alexandraya smirks and strokes his arm.

What is she playing at?

I move toward the edge of the Zen where an area is carved out for Electrical practice. There are two large boards placed next to each other with exposed wiring and bulbs on each. There is no one else in this space so I have it all to myself. I start concentrating, repeating the words learned in class, and point my finger at the first board. To my complete surprise, the bulb lights up. *Yes, success.* I am so proud of myself. I should have waited for Roman to join me so he could witness my triumph.

"So 'basic'." Davina shouts sarcastically.

I hadn't realised anyone was watching but I should have known better, the TON are always where I least expect. Their presence always intimidating and oppressive—an ombré of darkness with their varying shades of inky tresses.

"What do you guys want?" I reply a little too timidly.

"Stay away from Roman." Alexandraya directs in a tone full of malice, her deep emerald green eyes narrowing. "He's way above your league."

"Wha... what," I reply, the shock hitting me like a punch to the gut.

"We'd hate to see you end up face down in the Zen River, Siriarna," Alexandraya concludes. And with that, all three girls flick their hair in unison and stalk toward the learning rooms.

Images of Miriam lying face down in the river rush to my mind. Reliving the moment our class found her floating motionless sends shivers down my spine, despite the permanent tepid temperature of the realm.

Surely the TON's threat isn't bona fide?

Even though I'm doubtful, I decide it's best to skip practice and leave before Roman arrives.

Making my way to the Learning Facility, I take calculated steps staying on the pathway, while constantly looking over my shoulder. I tell myself I'm being ridiculous but then the murky image of Miriam's floating body enters my mind and I hasten my steps.

Entering the classroom, I see Roman seated in the middle of the room. I make my way toward the empty seat beside him, but Davina flies past and fills the spot before I have the chance. Alexandraya, already seated on Roman's other side, leans behind him and whispers, "Stay away, you've been warned."

With forced resignation, I continue to the front row and sit alone. The lecturer begins with an outline of today's practical lesson. He spies me in the front row and raises a brow—this is the class I normally ditch. But today I stay, remembering my promise to High Power Omnisensus, even though every bone in my body screams *run*.

"Pair up people," Lecturer Henrik instructs.

The enormity of the lesson starts to play on my mind, and I am frozen at my table, my limbs numb in panic.

"Siriarna, would you mind being my partner?"

My heart skips a beat as I turn expecting Roman. But it's not him. It's Braxton, the mysterious guy from the library who sits with Sixth Year Propensity students. Even though frowned upon, he doesn't seem to care about the rules, he's really quite reckless.

Clearing his throat, his keen chestnut brown eyes are

set on mine, waiting for a response. "Sure," I respond absently while scanning the room in search of Roman.

******

Braxton

She said yes! I've been trying to get her attention for ages, but she is always so engrossed in whatever she is reading. I know the crew I hang with are intimidating but they are the only people here on Evolirium who can help me reach my goal. I know others think I'm some kind of rebel, but I have cause.

The few times I've tried to get Siriarna's attention have fallen flat. I wish I could tell if she's noticed my ploys, but her thick wall of caramel hair hides her expression. Her shielded violet eyes I have only glimpsed on occasion when she distractedly sweeps her hair off her face in concentration. Today's class challenge is exactly the opportunity I have been hoping for. I smile my response, even though she isn't as excited as I am by our partnership.

*****

Siriarna

The lesson was way better than I had anticipated, my magic even made a short appearance. In fact, the class flew by, and I managed to get through the whole lesson relatively unscathed. I might go so far as to say I enjoyed it.

Lecturer Henrik asks Braxton to stay behind. Careful not to interrupt their conversation, I squeeze past and mouth 'thank you'. The grin I receive in return from Braxton is quite brilliant.

I turn in search of Roman, but the classroom is empty. Strange that he didn't wait for me. Moments later, I see why. He is standing on the pathway at the dorm entry point, animatedly speaking to the TON. All four are laughing and don't see me slip past.

Tears sting my eyes as I enter my darkened hut. Without flicking the switch the lights inside illuminate. But I can't bring myself to question what just happened because I am just so damn mad.

******

Alexandraya

I pray to the gods that Siriarna takes the not-so-subtle hint to leave Roman alone. He has grown so tall over the past two years, and if the rumours he is the son of an original Olympian are to be believed, he will be the perfect king to my realm-queen status.

"I think it's time to progress Plan A," I say to my loyal maidens.

Melodie responds with a resounding nod, and Davina agrees. "Absolutely."

"Ah girls, what would I do without you?" I laugh cherishing their devoted friendship. Today the girls are huddled on my couch while I sit in my velvet wingback chair. We could have congregated at any one of our huts, because they're all lined in a row, but I am most comfortable when I sit on my throne. "I think Roman was receptive, maybe a little sceptical? Thoughts ladies?"

Melodie speaks up, "Definitely receptive. He was laughing at everything you said."

"As if he can resist your charms." Davina adds.

And she's right!

"What about his devotion to Siriarna. We may have

scared her into backing off, but I'm not sure he will pull away so easily." Melodie adds.

"You leave that to me, by the end of this evening, I guarantee you it won't be an issue."

Hours later, I wrap my knuckles on a hut door located on the adjacent pathway.

"Just a second." Roman yells out groggily. "Alexandraya, what are you doing here? It's almost midnight," he says stifling a yawn.

"I'm just so panicked about tomorrow's Propensity Selections, I can't sleep. My Light magic isn't working properly and it's making me sick. I was hoping you might help me." I say in mock desperate tones.

"Come in." He widens the door opening. I have to bow my head so he can't see the triumph spread across my face.

I smooth my black negligee over my hips as I enter.

The Fates may not be listening to my relentless pleas to become a God, but I will make my own fate. I crave immortality, I was born for it. No one ignores me, no one.

CHAPTER 5

Siriarna

Today is Propensity Selections. The Zeneym Arena is brimming with activity. Immediately my nerves start to fray as I scan the arena. This year, there are forty-six eligible 18-year-old students, including myself, waiting to showcase. The enormity of today's magic display is steadily building, and I absently pierce my bottom lip with my teeth. Swiping the blood away with the back of my hand, I take a long deep breath, count to three, and release the air from my lungs in an attempt to refocus my energy.

Observing the six Propensity tents set up around the perimeter of the arena, butterflies form in the pit of my stomach threatening to break free at any given moment. The tents are marked, and I am hoping I qualify for at least one of them.

TIME — Red.
LIGHT – Yellow.
DARKNESS — Grey
WATER — Blue
EARTH — Green
ELECTRICITY — Purple

Taking me by surprise, a pair of arms circle my waist from behind and hot breath tickles my neck. Immediately, goose bumps prick my skin. "Sorry I missed you yesterday. Please forgive me." Roman whispers in my ear.

"It's fine."

"How are you feeling about your showcase?"

"I'm a complete wreck."

Roman plants a kiss on my cheek. "You'll be fine. Trust yourself and your magic will follow."

My cheeks turn crimson at his touch. "You're right, I'm going to nail this." I respond with a tight smile.

"That's the spirit." He easily scoops me up with one

arm and swirls me around until I'm dizzy.

"You're a big child, you know that."

"I do, and I know you love me for it."

Steadying my stance, I take my place at the end of the student line whilst I search the innermost depths of my soul to find some bravado.

Once my magic showcase is complete, a flag from each Propensity's Leader will be raised if they believe I would be a worthy addition to their group. It's then up to me to choose the Propensity (from the ones who raised their flags), that I am most drawn to. The problem is my sporadic magic. I'm petrified it won't cooperate and no flags will be raised. The nausea returns to my stomach.

The commencement horn blasts, indicating the tests are to begin. All excited chatter in the arena ceases as the seriousness of this process commences.

Alexandraya strides toward the light pillars.

"Of course, *she* is the first student showcasing," I turn to Roman and roll my eyes, but his eyes are glued to her silhouette.

With a raspy voice, Alexandraya begins a chant and is straight into bending light between the pillars. She is moving them so effortlessly from one to another, changing their colour and shape. Much to my annoyance, it is fascinating to watch. She moves through the next five Propensity's with the same superior skill. It is no surprise all six Group Leaders raise their flags. I'm sure she'll choose Time; it is the hardest Propensity to get accepted into and the most prestigious. I'm utterly gobsmacked when she selects Light.

At the conclusion of today's selections, each Propensity will study together leaving little time to socialise with anyone outside their Prop. I always assumed Roman and I would end up separated after the selections. As it draws closer, I'm left with that bleak reality.

It is Braxton's turn to showcase. Darkness descends the Zen in a split second. It is quickly brightened following a snap to Light. He finishes all six showcases in record speed, producing a brilliant display in each. It doesn't surprise me because he is the only other student who spends nearly as much time as I do in the Knowledge Room. His Propensity selection is Time, and a smile lifts the corner of my mouth.

The remaining students complete their showcase, and I can hide no longer. I must perform. I tentatively step toward the centre of the arena and attempt to stop Time for the required five seconds. Chanting the words, the five twisted ribbons of Time appear in my palm. I select the ribbon that relates to Evolirium and gradually twist it as we were taught in class. Nothing happens, time moves pace as normal. Utter fail!

I promptly move on to Earth and the alchemy showcase, trying to forget my ill-fated start. I stand in front of the centrally placed table and select a beaker. Then, I carefully pluck ingredients from the assortment of herbs placed around the table and add them to the beaker. Next, I place my selected mix into a mortar and pestle and grind to a smooth paste. I add elixir, stir, and chant. A smoke-like rope is supposed to appear to manipulate. My potion makes a pathetic puff that barley leaves the bowl—another lacklustre display. My only relief is all other students are so involved with their new Props and peers, no one is interested in watching me. Apart from Roman—gods, bless him. I glance over. He is giving me a thumbs up signal, encouraging me from the sidelines.

I make my way to the edge of the Zen River to showcase Water. It starts well. I manage to get the stream flowing quickly and I am, finally, gaining confidence. I try to raise a wave, but the stream is just too fast. I can't get the water to rise. I can't slow it down either. With a panic, I cast too much power resulting in the formation of a mini tidal wave. And, as fast as it appears, it hastily descends, crashing down over the Light Propensity tent with force. Students not directly underneath are now saturated. Alexandraya was not under the tent. She is now dripping wet and seething, her eyes flashing with anger—I have completely ruined her white training uniform, which is now showing signs of see-through. Her hair is hanging limply around her face, water trickling down her skin. She is staring at me with such hostility. *As if she didn't already hate me.*

Trying to put the recent disaster out of my mind, I move to Light and then to Darkness. Both are a bust. I did manage to bend the light and darken the Zen but for a mere snap only and neither were impressive.

My last performance is Electricity. I stand between the electrical boards, chant and cast my spells toward them. Nothing. Frustration engulfs me because this is the one Propensity I focussed my practice on. Fuming, I make one last attempt and as I cast my spell, one light bulb on the first board shines. It illuminated before I finished the chant. *How weird.*

My showcase has now concluded and it was a disaster. I am not expecting any flags. But one *is* raised—Electricity. I did it. I have a Propensity. I'm in!

I turn to Roman. He is clearly thrilled and gives me a distant air high five.

******

Braxton

Standing alone in the corner of the Time Propensity tent, I am watching Siriarna's showcase with keen interest. I'd be lying if I said I didn't want her to succeed and select Time Propensity, just as I did. Unfortunately, the abominable showcase will likely land her without Propensity and likely see her leaving the realm completely. This thought pulls at my heart, and I wonder if anyone would notice if I manipulated time to allow her a redo? I know it is a skill that I am not supposed to yet possess but my friends in Sixth Year have been sharing their spells and instruction—for a price of course; one I am more than willing to pay.

Turning my back to avoid being seen, I covertly summon the Time ribbons to my palm. Just as I am about to act, I spy a raised flag from the corner of my eye. Siriarna has been selected. *Well, I'll be damned.*

******

Siriarna

Roman is the last student to showcase. He confidently strolls to each station and performs with such direct ease. All the students are watching him from their tents with piqued interest, a courtesy not afforded to myself. He finishes his round with his favourite skill, Light. The colours he conjures are magnificent, not the average range but an assortment of shades, bright and shimmering. The crowd erupts in cheer and all flags are risen. It is no surprise he walks directly into the Light tent. Straight into Alexandraya's arms—now that was a surprise I didn't see coming, and one I do not like. *Not one tiny bit.* It suddenly makes sense why she chose the Light Propensity. Jealousy flicks around my stomach, and I try my best to quash it.

High Power Omnisensus moves to the top of the

tower located in the middle of the Propensity tents. His voice echoes around the arena. "Congratulations to everyone selected today. I am proud of you all."

This was supposed to be a moment of glory, but I'm not listening. I'm thinking about Roman. *Why he is suddenly so into Alexandraya? He has always agreed with me that she is way too self-absorbed, even for a semi god.*

"It is time for you to embrace your Propensity and celebrate your impending future," continues the Authority.

In the centre of each Propensity tent, small cylindrical vials are spread across a table. Each vial contains a liquid.

"Drink," he proclaims.

Along with all students, I take a vial and guzzle the contents in one sip. Spell casting index fingers are now stained with the colour pertaining to an individual's Propensity. Mine is purple. Group Leaders hand around new uniforms, coloured in Propensity, to replace our former white training uniform.

"The anointment is complete. Let the celebration commence," beams High Power Omnisensus.

Goddess Iris shoots through the air on her chariot throwing a rainbow over the skies of Evolirium. The sound of cheering fills the Zen as the enormity of today's selections sink in. I silently thank the Fates.

Finally, my wishes have been answered.

Now in a celebratory mood, I scan the Light Propensity tent in search of Roman. My gaze finds instead Alexandraya, who has a huge smile plastered across her face. Upon closer inspection, I see her hand in Roman's. *They're holding hands.*

Simeon, the Electrical Group Leader, approaches and somehow I manage to pull myself together. "That was some display out there Siriarna."

"Um, thanks."

"You don't realise what you just did, do you?"

"I lit a bulb."

A deep throaty chuckle escapes his lips. "Yes Siriarna, you lit the bulb. What you don't realise is that you did it through thought, not with a chant or spell. No one else saw. It was so quick, I only just caught it myself. You must not speak of this to anyone...yet. Do you understand?"

"Okay." I reply grateful to be in this Propensity, regardless of how I got here.

CHAPTER 6

Siriarna

I wake before dawn, stretch out my body and grin, the significance of my Propensity achievement still fresh. After changing into my new purple uniform, I dance around my hut humming before collapsing onto my couch laughing. Catching my breath, I think about the other students. *Will they like me?*

To make sure there's no awkward entrances, I arrive at our meeting point early. Not long after, I hear distant chatter approaching as my new group members appear. Some of us have had classes together in the past, but there are two members who I have not worked with before—Eloise and Mykos. The banter is easy-going and friendly—

a glimmer of optimism washes over me.

Leader Simeon arrives and shepherds us to our new classroom. "Team, this will be your permanent fixture for the next year. You are about to embark upon the first of the designated six year Propensity training. At its conclusion, you will have a choice to make. Whilst I know it's quite some time away, you might want to start considering your futures. With hard work, some of you may even become members of The Core."

"That's my life goal," Mykos blurts out. His thickset body and near-black eyes animate when he speaks.

"I dream about being a part of that group," Eloise says enchanted.

For me, thinking about The Core makes my pulse quicken. An elite amalgamated Propensity group who tackle intricate missions and liaise directly with the gods; it's a semi god's highest achievement. A most coveted and highly competitive position.

Could this really be my future? Stefanie would be ridiculously proud. I shudder at the thought of future masquerade parties if I did make The Core.

Simeon cuts into my daydream, "Today, we start with the theory of Electricity."

A loud bang echoes around the room as he drops a huge encyclopedia onto the table with a clunk. A collective groan reverberates around the room, but I am secretly thrilled because I have already read and memorised this entire encyclopedia.

The rest of the week goes by without any issues. With a small class, study and practice are easy to complete. We are more than halfway through the encyclopedia and as I already know its entire content, I have been able to concentrate on practical lessons. My skills are improving too. I can now light a bulb quickly with a chant and a flick of my purple finger, the colour perfectly matching my eyes. I'm positive it is a sign of great things to come.

The only thing missing from my life right now is Roman. We are so busy with our new Props, there hasn't been any time to hang out. As we are no longer in the same class and end times vary, we haven't been walking home together like we used to. I miss it. I miss *him*.

"Wait up Siriarna," Roman yells out.

Fast as the speed of light, he is standing beside me.

"Hey, Roman," I reply solemnly. "I was just thinking about you."

"All good things I'm sure," he winks.

"Um... yes." I stutter, my cheeks turning crimson.

Oh gods, I sound ridiculous. I hope he doesn't notice.

If he does, he doesn't say anything. He just keeps on chatting, casually dropping into the conversation, "Do you think we could talk this afternoon?"

Here it is. The moment I've been dreading ever since the Anointment Ceremony. I know reading minds isn't a skill we possess as semi gods; that is a gift the Fates have only bestowed on certain gods, but it doesn't take a special skill to know exactly what he wants to talk about. *Alexandraya.*

We reach my hut and I invite Roman in for a mountain elixir. A huge exhalation of pent-up breath escapes his lips as he rushes to open the door for me.

"So, um, well, here's the thing. It's about Alexandraya. She's kind of my girlfriend."

He has always hated the TON, so why on Evolirium was he dating the queen of bullies herself?

It just doesn't make any sense.

My heartbeat accelerates at the thought of them together. Before I can form a response, the lights in my hut flick on, then abruptly shatter into thousands of pieces. The sound is terrifying. Roman dives over the top of me to protect me from the falling shards of glass.

"Siriarna, are you okay? What just happened?"

"I think you'd better leave now Roman," I say wriggling from underneath him.

Like the lightbulbs, my heart splinters into just as many pieces.

"I won't leave you here like this, you're shaking like a leaf. You're my best friend and I need to make sure you're okay."

"If I really was your best friend Roman, you wouldn't be dating Alexandraya. You know how I feel about her. What happened to Friends First Always?" I retort.

"Oh, she's not that bad Siriarna, she's changed. Honest. I know you've had some issues, but I also know that it's all in the past now. Trust me. And we are friends always."

I am crestfallen at the absence of 'first'. Our two-year friendship is dissolving before my eyes. "Go home Roman, I don't want to speak to you right now."

He tries to protest, but once he catches my sullen face, walks straight to the door, shoulders slumped.

After his departure, I collapse onto my bed in sheer frustration and close my eyes. I have developed a throbbing headache.

What I really should have done was analyse the lightbulb situation. This was the third time I manipulated electricity with my mind and, this time it was dangerous.

CHAPTER 7

Siriarna

To take my mind off the whole Roman and Alexandraya fiasco, I throw myself into my practical skills training. Before dawn breaks each morning, I meet Simeon at the electrical boards for additional tuition. I hardly pay attention to the early hour rise time, my body now acclimatised to its new routine.

Focussing on my abilities has had a double effect. Firstly, I have less time to dwell on the fact that Roman is spending all his time with Alexandraya. And secondly, my magic has started to improve, which is an unexpected bonus. It is nowhere near as good as the other four first year students in my Propensity, but I can hold my own in practical classes now. The only downside of this extra training has been the headaches that are appearing more frequently, although they are a small price to pay.

Today, we are taking a field trip into the mountains. The other students have been excitedly discussing this trip for weeks now, but I haven't really given it a second thought. I'm losing track of time because all my days are passing quickly—classes, extra training, and sleeping; then repeat, day in day out.

Walking through the centre of the Zeneym Arena to the river dock, I spy the yellow training uniforms of the Light Propensity class working on their skills at the light pillars. My heart lurches at the sight of Roman, but I avert my eyes quickly hoping he doesn't catch me staring. Head down, I board the vessel that will float down the shallow waters of the river, taking us directly to the base of the mountain.

Normally I love cruising through the realm by boat, gazing at the changing landscapes from the wildflower filled meadows, to the dense treescape of the Ovallium Forest. But during this trip, I glare aimlessly at the scenery, distracted by the prior sight of Roman in the Zen.

The hustle from the other students departing the

watercraft jolts me from my thoughts. Slowly I rise, blink my eyes into focus, and join my Propensity on the riverbank.

"Follow me," Simeon announces.

Our Propensity Leader sets off, expertly negotiating his way up the narrow, winding mountainside track. He makes it look easy, but I struggle to find my footing and slip on the uneven, rocky terrain. Astrid reaches down and helps me regain my footing, and together we persevere to the top. The higher we climb, the cooler the temperature.

By the time we reach the rest of the group at the peak, the climate is freezing. Goosebumps prick my flesh in my short-sleeved purple training uniform. Astrid wraps her arms around her body, Eloise is fidgeting from foot to foot, while Frasier and Mykos are briskly rubbing their flesh to encourage blood flow.

"As you can all feel, it's cold up here," Simeon says, his warm breath creating little smoky puffs. "Today's field trip emulates a possible scenario on the Surface World where you must create heat using your abilities."

Eloise stammers through chattering teeth, "I can't remember the chant."

"Work together. We will not be leaving until you can

all create an electrical spark and start a fire. I will be watching from these boulders." Simeon announces, pointing to the cluster of rocks behind us. He puts on a warm over jacket, and moves to takes his place.

"I guess we should start." Eloise squeaks.

"I'll gather some firewood with Astrid. You guys clear a space while we're gone," suggests Mykos taking charge.

He and Astrid take off in a hurry and return a short time later with arms full of sticks and larger branches. They dump the material into the cleared space, and with cold, stiff fingers, arrange each piece into a fire base. Then the group forms a circle around the perimeter in preparation for the chant. I find myself getting wrapped up in the excitement of the simulated Surface World test despite the chilled air.

Eloise is in full panic mode now. She is fidgeting on the spot, kicking up dirt and mumbling away. Mykos, Frasier, and Astrid are staring at the branches, shivering.

"Does anyone remember the spell?" Astrid asks desperately.

"I do," I reply calmly, and everyone snaps their attention to me, impressed.

"Well, what is it?" Mykos asks abruptly.

I begin to recite the spell from memory. Before I get to the final words, Mykos swoops in finishing my chant and casting his purple finger at the firewood. A small spark ignites the kindling, and a flame catches one of the branches. Frasier, Eloise and Astrid jump in and cast their spells, successfully adding additional flames to the now blazing firewood.

The heat offers an instant reprieve and the team stand around the fire admiring their Propensity handiwork. Mykos is preening, announcing he led the success. My eyes narrow to a squint.

Amongst the celebration, Frasier signals Simeon who is already striding his way over. "Congratulations Electrical Propensity."

Mykos turns to leave and the rest of the group follow behind on a magic-high from their training success. No one seems aware that I haven't had a chance to cast my spell. I glance at the firewood wistfully before joining the others. Behind our backs, a resounding crack erupts as the firewood turns into a raging inferno.

"Oh my gods, look what we did," Astrid cries out.

Simeon reaches into his pocket and pulls out a pouch from the Alchemy Laboratory. He scoops up a handful of dust and scatters it over the blaze, extinguishing the flames. I catch the raised eye in my direction as he joins the group.

Did I do that?

I think about the flames on the way back to the Learning Facility. I know Simeon thinks I had something to do with the mini explosion, but I honestly don't know how I could have. Surely it was the combination of the four electrical sparks created by my peers?

Upon our return, I notice the Zen is empty and Roman's Propensity is no longer training. I really wish I could talk to him about what happened today. I toy with the idea of going straight to his hut, but the possibility of bumping into Alexandraya, immediately vetoes that idea.

I resign myself instead to a long hot steamy bath and an early night to try and relax my tangled thoughts.

CHAPTER 8

Siriarna

Rising early the next morning, I head straight to the Knowledge Room. On my way through the hallway, I pass High Power Omnisensus' office and overhear raised voices. The resonating tone indicates the Authority is speaking to a god. I know I should continue toward my destination, but my curiosity takes hold and I stop, pressing my ear against the door.

"The situation on the Surface World has escalated. The message is that you must act now. Zeus wants the new students sent in to see what they are made of," states Hermes, the most trusted messenger of Mt Olympus.

"I don't believe the new Propensity students are

ready," sighs High Power Omnisensus.

The conversation has halted and the sound of footsteps moving closer to the door I am leaning against, makes my heartbeat race. I move backward only catching bits and pieces of the remaining conversation.

"In that case, I will disperse a group from The Core to act as a backup team. They will only intercede if necessary and will keep a low profile. I don't want the first-year students knowing they have help on hand," commands Hermes.

A golden flash of light shoots under the doorway signalling Hermes has left Evolirium. I make a hasty retreat to ensure I don't get caught snooping.

Before Simeon commences today's lesson, an announcement orb zips into the classroom at light speed directing all first year Propensity students to the Grand Auditorium.

Students are mingling, chatting, and guesstimating why we have been summoned. I see Roman and the TON enter together. He tries to catch my eye, but I pretend I haven't seen him in the crowd, even though with his height, he is hard to miss. Instead, I turn sideways to Eloise and strike up small talk.

From the corner of my eye, I watch Roman's shoulders drop. The disappointment at the way things were left between us a couple of weeks ago plays on my mind. But much as I want to, I can't bring myself to deal with him right now. I am conflicted because I want to rush over and pretend all is well in the realm, but I just can't process that he is quite literally, sleeping with my enemy.

"Please, take a seat everyone," instructs High Power Omnisensus.

All forty-six students move toward the chairs, neatly placed in rows.

The Authority clears his throat and begins. "The great Hermes has delivered us a mission to Earth."

A loud, simultaneous gasp fills the room. Then, all students start chatting excitedly at once.

"Silence," he booms.

All eyes are fixated on the Authority as he continues, "There is a situation on the Surface World that we must take care of immediately. Earth's core has been compromised and needs our intervention. A team will be created to undertake this mission. Instructions have been given to your Propensity Leaders. They will explain further steps and actions. I need everyone to stay calm.

Selected semi gods are to prepare for immediate departure. Go now."

Students make a beeline to their Propensity Leaders in a stampede, completely ignoring the Authority's keep calm instruction.

Avoiding the compounding chaos that has eventuated, Simeon weaves our small group from the Auditorium. Once in our classroom, he leads the discussions with an outline of the mission. Two candidates from each Propensity will form the mission team and will attempt to heal the Earth's core at the source. If unsuccessful, all mortals within the vicinity are to be evacuated. It is a huge task and one not to be taken lightly.

All five Electrical First Year Propensity members, including myself, look solemnly at Simeon with nervous energy. The mission is dangerous and unexpected for our first, but the honour of being selected is at the forefront of all our minds. I know I will not be part of the electrical pair heading to the Surface World. Whilst my skills have improved, I do not have the same level of control the other members do. With this knowledge, I breathe a sigh of relief. I know I'm not ready.

All eyes are focused on Simeon; Mykos hasn't blinked

since we entered the classroom.

"I have selected both Mykos and Siriarna. Both of you are to return to your huts, pack a light satchel of belongings and meet in the Knowledge Room immediately."

He leads by example and moves through the room.

"Yes Sir," Mykos gloats and immediately follows, leaving me standing dumbstruck and awkward amongst the remaining Propensity members.

"Would you consider sending me, Sir?" Frasier asks desperately.

His request is unheard because Simeon is no longer in the room.

I glance at Eloise and Astrid–their faces say it all. They are furious.

"Hey guys, I'm not sure why I was chosen," I say nervously.

"Of course you do, Siriarna," replies Astrid.

"I really don't, please don't be angry," I beg.

"Always privately chatting with Simeon. Getting extra lessons every morning behind all our backs," Frasier spits into the conversation.

"That's not true, I am only asking for help to keep up

with the rest of you guys," I respond. *And to keep my thoughts from pining for Roman.*

"It *is* true what everyone says about you Siriarna. Not only are you magic basic, but you are also a liar. From now on, stay away from us," Eloise fumes.

With that, my remaining three Propensity members turn their backs in succession and storm out. I am left standing alone in the middle of the classroom.

******

Returning to the Knowledge Room with my satchel packed, I find Simeon waiting at the top of the spiral staircase. As I approach, I am mid-sentence asking why he selected me for this mission. He simply raises his hand and I stop my speech.

"Siriarna," he starts anticipating my question. "You have read the entire encyclopedia on all things Electricity," he continues.

"So, what?" I shrug.

"You have more knowledge than any other Propensity member and your powers are strengthening every day. I witnessed the way you remembered the chant on the mountain field trip, and the way you kept your composure. You will be an asset to Mykos and the entire group."

Conversation over, he descends the staircase to the Reading Hub.

I'm not sure I agree with his assessment. I am nervous, but a spark of excitement tingles through my body at the prospect of entering another realm.

As I descend the staircase, I see all other Propensities are represented by their coloured training uniforms spread throughout the space. Each chosen member, together with their Group Leader, is sitting on the couches awaiting further instruction from High Power Omnisensus. I am the last to arrive.

My excitement at seeing Roman is soon extinguished. Alexandraya is the other member of the Light Propensity. *I should have known she would be here.*

She catches my eye, smirks, and rubs her leg against Roman's. It sickens me to watch, so I avert my gaze to the other Propensity representatives. Our motley group consists of twelve Semi Gods: Mykos and I from Electricity; Roman and Alexandraya from Light; Leister and Henry from Darkness; Julius and Brooklyn from

Water; Thea and Rebecka from Earth and, finally, Braxton and Sage from Time.

I settle my gaze on Braxton and start to relax, thankful for a friendly face.

"Thank you for your quick response everyone," commences High Power Omnisensus as I take my seat.

"You will be transported to a safe house located close to Niagara Falls in the third continent. According to the all-seeing Oracle, there is a crack at the very core of the Earth, leaking toxic fluids. If the liquid reaches the surface, the atmospheric pressure will cause an explosion. The crack lies beneath the whirlpool at the base of the falls. You have five days to complete your mission.

"As this is your first time travelling through the vortex, directly leading into a mission, you will need to manage your realm transition quickly and combat the travel lag. Ensure you blend into the mortal society, and any powers used remain undetected."

He hands each of us a vial of liquid on a chain. "The Alchemy Laboratory has prepared a communication elixir. This liquid can be used to signal each other in matters of urgency, unforeseen circumstances, or in case you become separated. It is also a direct link through the realms, able to reach me here on Evolirium. Drink the liquid and chant the words 'let me see what will be' and add the name of the person you wish to communicate with. It will bring a small communication orb into your palm. Be aware, the magic only lasts a minute or two so be hasty in your messages. Each of you will carry one vial. Use them wisely, work as a team. Remember to save a vial to indicate the completion of your mission and set about your return.

"Good luck and may the gods be with you."

Instructions complete, he clicks his fingers summoning a chariot to meet the group in the outer rim of the Zen.

Students and leaders are standing together when the chariot arrives. It is drawn by four divinely dappled-shaded immortal horses who come to an immediate standstill directly in front of us. The charioteer launches a ladder over the side of the vessel and instructs our group to board.

With a final salute from the six Propensity Leaders, the chariot departs, taking flight swiftly. Within minutes we are whisked into the idle darkness of the Vortex.

Our first mission has now commenced.

CHAPTER 9

Siriarna

In a mere snap, we are landing in a realm none of us have ever visited. The chariot is shrouded in a misty veil of glamour. The veil keeps our arrival hidden from the mortals of the Surface World.

The journey was quicker than I had expected, and it takes a moment for my eyes to adjust from the darkness of the vortex to the brightness of the Surface World.

"Whoa, what a ride," Mykos voices shaking his head, a huge grin spread across his face.

"Oh my gods above. This place is surreal." Brooklyn says in awe as the chariot departs and the glamour veil dissipates.

We are standing on a smooth concrete pathway, shadowed by a stone clad high-rise apartment building directly in front of us.

Despite Evolirium being modelled to deeply resemble the Surface World, for ease of adaption when performing missions, I am struck by the differences immediately. The towering height of the surrounding buildings being the most significant.

"You must be the Evolirium group," says a rather small lady standing at the entrance of the 12-storey building.

"We are," Alexandraya answers.

"Come in, come in," she says, ushering us into the building. "My name is Catherine Lowe, and I will be your mortal guide here on Earth. I have separate rooms for each of you over the top three floors—four individual rooms on each floor. They are shrouded in glamour as is the private elevator behind me. No one will see you nor disturb your business while you're here."

We decide to split the Propensities into Light and Darkness residing on the top floor, Earth and Water the level below, and Time and Electricity on the 10th floor.

"Isn't it weird hearing someone with two names?" muses Thea out loud to the group.

Catherine Lowe responds with a chuckle.

Our single name follows our godly genealogy. It is to remind us of our semi god status, and to ensure we do not become emotionally attached to our magically absent mortal lineage. For the first time, I think about my mortal birth parent and what my last name would have been.

Alexandraya speaks out interrupting the conversation, appointing herself spokesperson for the mission. "We should begin our reconnaissance of Niagara Falls as soon as we've settled into our rooms and changed into our street clothing," she says matter-of-factly.

Roman is hasty to nod, as are the rest of group.

Once in my temporary lodging, I throw my satchel onto the bed and riffle through the minimal clothing I bought with me. I decide on a pair of jeans and a simple plain white tee. Comfortable and non-descript. *Perfect.* I hurriedly run a brush through my hair, combing my vortex-swept bangs into place before I leave to meet the group.

"Right, that's everyone *now*," Alexandraya says to our guide while throwing a look of distaste in my direction.

"Follow me and I'll show you the way to the falls." Catherine Lowe instructs.

Mykos sidles up to Alexandraya and leaves me at the back of the group. *Traitor! Is anyone immune to her charms?*

"Hey, can you believe this place?"

It's Braxton walking by my side, engaging me in conversation.

"I can't get my head around the fact that I'm actually part of this group," I respond.

"Why do you say that?"

"Because I'm not as confident in my abilities as the rest of you," I reply simply.

"You really don't give yourself enough credit. You are quite remarkable."

Did he just call me remarkable? I turn my head toward the ground as my cheeks flush, and hide a little smile to myself.

"Here we are," Catherine Lowe says depositing us at a deserted vantage point. "I'll leave you lot to it. Just follow this pathway when you're done. It will lead you straight back to the apartments."

The first thing that catches my eye is the sheer power of the cascading water flow. The thunderous crash of water into the whirlpool below is both menacing and bewitching. It is the absolute opposite of the peaceful Zen River on Evolirium.

As the reality of the mission starts to sink in, my nerves bubble away inside my stomach. I look to Braxton wide-eyed. He nods, understanding my trepidation and gives me a little reassuring smile.

"Hey Siriarna, what are all these people wearing?" Thea asks interrupting my building anxiety.

Dragging my view from the waterfall, I look at the crowds instead, then answer, "Raincoats. Mortals wear them to keep their under clothes dry."

"Fascinating," she says, continuing to eyeball the mortal garments.

Though trivial, answering Thea's question lifts my spirits. Perhaps Simeon was right, and I can be of some help during this mission after all.

Alexandraya positions herself at the front of the group. "Time to split up and investigate. Roman and I will go with Sage, Thea, Julius and Mykos. We'll explore the best way to get to the bottom of the waterfall. The rest of you scope the area for an evacuation strategy in case of a mission fail. Let's meet back here at dusk."

I clear my throat before announcing my suggestion,

"There's a tunnel at the bottom of the power station. It should lead directly to the base of the falls."

"How do you know that?" Alexandraya snaps.

"I read the pamphlet in our accommodation before we left," I add modestly.

"No wonder you were late, *again*."

Roman jumps in and says, "Thanks Siriarna, we'll check it out."

Alexandraya flicks her hair while turning, and storms from our meeting into the crowds. "Well ..." she yells at her nominated team—they right away scurry after her.

Mortal tourists openly gape at her as she nears. I guess they're only human.

The remaining six of us turn in the opposite direction, away from the crowds.

"Looks like it's you and me again," Braxton says.

I return his statement with a smile.

"We're lucky you're here, Siriarna. How do you remember all that information?"

"It's easy. Well, for me it is. I don't know how to explain it properly, but once I read something, the information somehow sticks in my mind forever," I answer.

"That's an amazing gift you have."

"Thanks. I guess it is."

Braxton's conversation and interest in my knowledge retention is a nice distraction from my building nerves. The impending use of my physical powers is churning at the pit of my stomach. I concentrate instead on the task of finding a relocation point.

We scout the surrounding precinct and take note of the number of tourists, buses and private vehicles stationed in the parking area. Opposite, and an easy flat walk from the attraction, is a huge open green space with enough room to initially relocate a substantial amount of people. The six of us agree this would be an excellent place to hoard the mortals if needed. Hopefully, it won't be.

Completing our assessment, we regroup at the designated meeting point. Alexandraya's group is already waiting. She shoots me an icy glare as I approach, and I take a sideways step closer to Braxton.

Collectively, we decide it's best to assess the crack in the Earth's core under the cloak of darkness, where we will have less chance of being spotted using our powers. Thea slyly mentions that the power station is how we'll navigate our way!

Following the pathway as Catherine Lowe instructed, we easily find our way back to the apartment block.

Roman sidles up beside me. "Hey, you," he says a little sheepishly.

"Hi," I respond. It's all I can come up with.

"Can we talk?" he asks in almost a whisper.

"Okay."

"We'll catch up with you guys a bit later," Roman yells to the rest of our group.

Alexandraya's eyes close to a sliver, however, she continues to lead the group inside the apartment block. Braxton nods in my direction and disappears ahead.

Roman grabs my hand and leads me to an empty bench in the adjacent park. As we sit in the late afternoon twilight, the lamppost above flickers to life. "I've missed you Siriarna. Can we please call a truce and get back to normal?" he asks.

I smile and respond with a conceding shrug, "I guess we can try."

He reaches across and wraps me in a bear hug. The gesture causes me a swift intake of breath, yet it is familiar and comforting. Butterflies circle inside my stomach, and at this very moment, I decide I will not let Alexandraya come between us.

CHAPTER 10

Siriarna

Early the next morning, the group meet on the twelfth floor of the apartment building in Alexandraya's room.

Before we use a communication vial to contact High Power Omnisensus, Alexandraya appoints herself spokesperson. She insists there isn't enough time to waste with multiple personal recounts. Scanning the room, it seems no one has a problem with her barking orders.

After swigging the contents of the liquid vial, Alexandraya chants the communication spell. Within moments, the Authority's image materialises within the translucent mist. "Sir, we have discovered the Winter Solstice will be in three days and think this will be our best chance to heal the core, due to the extended nightfall. We'll do some more reconnaissance this realm evening," she relays.

"Hello everyone. Continue as planned. Keep me in the loop—"

The magic lapses and the Authority's image fades away.

******

"We've got hours before nightfall, perhaps we should take some time out to look around town and explore," suggests Alexandraya. "Do not go alone. Everyone must ensure they have another semi god with them for safety purposes. And make sure you keep your coloured finger out of plain sight," she commands.

All eleven group members hastily agree, including myself. I am super keen to explore the Surface Realm.

Catherine Lowe suggests the Main Street Marketplace as a tourist destination. This recommendation appeals to most of the group, and we head out with rowdy enthusiasm.

The streets are a flurry of activity with crowds of

people mingling in and out of the vibrant stalls. All are brimming with activity and an overflow of tourists. One stall, at the end of the block and hidden behind much larger tents, displays a faded, dusty banner reading 'Ms M Clairvoyant'. The stall is empty, but I find myself intrigued by the space. The other group members are nowhere to be seen, and I hesitate before entering. But a voice from within draws me closer.

"Come now dear, take a seat." An elderly lady with snow white hair scraped into a bun, beckons.

I follow her request and sit opposite. "Are you Ms M?" I ask.

"Yes, my dear. Give me your hands." She instructs gently.

I clench my fists and thrust them into my jean pockets, wondering if I should get up and leave.

"There is no need to hide your coloured finger, I know you are not of this realm."

My eyes widen and my pulse quickens. Ms M lets out a low chuckle. "Now, your hands please."

Timidly, I place both hands in Ms M's. She closes her eyes and asks me to do the same. "I can feel your energy, semi god."

I take a deep breath in. "I'm not sure what to do." I say.

"Just relax and keep breathing, dear. When your mind is clear, I will be able to penetrate your barriers and glimpse your destiny."

Behind closed eyelids, I continue to breathe until my chest rises and falls in a hypnotic rhythm. I drift into a state of consciousness between wakefulness and slumber.

Ms M's voice sounds distant, and I need to focus my concentration to hear her words.

"A great journey awaits, one you cannot hide from," she conveys.

All of a sudden she drops my hands, and they crash onto the table, instantly dragging me out of the dreamlike state.

"What's wrong?" I ask, my voice shaking from the traumatic wakening.

"There is a deep energy blocking your ability. Once your mind is clear, your psychokinesis will surface."

My eyes fill with tears, hidden behind a sheath of hair. *Psychokinesis?* Urgently, I ask, "How can I unblock this energy?"

"That I cannot tell you, only you hold the key. When you truly awaken, so will your power. Leave now child."

Ms M stands and scurries out the back of her tent stall.

Could she be right? Is this why I am able to use magic through thought? And why the sudden departure?

The air is thick with smog as I make my way through the inner streets on my way back to the apartments. I keep walking, not taking any notice of where I am, while I digest the possibility of possessing psychokinesis. It is a daunting prospect, and it unnerves me.

Hours pass and the sky is morphing from hues of burnt oranges to moody aubergine. My thoughts trail to God Apollo as the sun slips from the sky. The streets are deserted as dusk turns to twilight, and they all begin to look the same. It's now that I remember I shouldn't be alone.

With the fading light, my panic grows—I have no idea where the apartment is or how to get there. I start walking briskly in the opposite direction, hoping to jog my memory on which streets led me here. Nope. Nothing. They all look the same–high-rise buildings and endlessly long streets.

I wonder if the group will notice my absence.

Will they leave for the mission without me?

The rising panic begins to engulf me. My hands reach

for the vial around my neck, and I drink, "let me see what will be," I chant. I have every intention of speaking Roman's name, but Braxton's is the one that passes my lips.

His profile appears right away, "Siriarna, where are you? Are you alright?" he asks with an edge to voice.

"Actually, Braxton, I'm a bit lost."

"Don't worry, I'll find you. Stay exactly where you are and keep talking—"

Within seconds, Braxton is at my side. A lucky break because the communication mirror in my hand faded mid-sentence.

"How did you find me so fast?"

"Easy, I turned back Time, and followed you from the Marketplace."

"Why can't I remember any of it?"

"Time is tricky. Only the manipulator and Realm Master have the ability to retain the memory. It allows us to pass through timespans succinctly."

How fascinating. I am starting to understand why only the elite students are accepted into this Propensity.

"Come on," he nudges me in the ribs. "Let's get back before anyone notices our absence."

"Thank you, Braxton... for finding me."

He dramatizes a bow and replies, "It is a pleasure, my lady."

I like the way that sounds. *'My lady,'* I wordlessly repeat, smiling.

******

Braxton

The look on Siriarna's face is the same one that appears on my guide mother's face after my guide father has been drinking stolen nectar from the gods. I know she's putting on brave face, but her eyes tell a different story.

I won't push her into sharing her dilemma. Instead, I will make sure I am the safe space she needs, ready to listen when her time is right.

For now, I'm thrilled she used her communication vial to summon me. I will always make myself available for her.

******

Siriarna

Darkness has now enveloped the realm. By some complete miracle, Braxton and I make it back to the apartments in time for the mission. With no time to second guess myself, I throw on my black mission uniform before joining the other semi gods in the foyer. Catching Braxton's eye amongst the group already gathered, I smile my relief and he nods in response. *We made it.*

Now assembled, we head out to the whirlpool at the base of Niagara Falls. Predictably, Alexandraya is out in front, leading the group. To be fair, even though I don't want to be, she has conjured a ball of light to illuminate our journey. For that matter, so has Roman, who is walking at her side.

The light makes for an easier passage, especially when we reach the power station. Mykos zaps the chained gates with electricity breaking the lock, and we are now able to enter the facility. Leister throws a cloud of darkness over the security cameras, and Mykos zaps the alarm system before I have the chance to use my Propensity power.

Once inside, Alexandraya takes control, "Follow me— at the end of this hallway is a maintenance shaft that will lead us directly to the tunnel below."

Arriving at the shaft, Roman throws his ball of light into the depths of the cavernous space and Sage suspends it in time, creating our own magical lantern.

The gleam highlights steep, rusty ladders bolted precariously to the facility's limestone wall. The sight causes me involuntary paralysis. Not so for Mykos, he hurtles down the first ladder which remains steady, despite its first appearance. The others follow behind leaving only Braxton and I to descend.

"Ladies first."

"I can't do it, Braxton." I say frozen in place.

He moves to my side, picks up my limp hand and says, "Let's do this together."

I nod, trying to find a tiny ounce of bravery, which is proving difficult.

"Let's take a step forward, okay? On the count of three," he says. "One, two—"

He moves forward before finishing the countdown. Automatically, my body responds by following. "Hey, you cheated." I lightly scold. Secretly I'm thrilled. It was exactly the jolt I needed.

Now, I've made the first step, the process of climbing

down the ladder doesn't seem as daunting. "I think I'll take you up on your offer and go first if that's okay?"

"Absolutely," he grins.

My legs follow the rungs effortlessly, and I reach the ground below safely. Braxton right behind me. *What was I worried about?*

Reunited with the rest of the group, we wordlessly move through the tunnel's wide passageway. At the exit, we come face to face with a river that snakes its way to the base of the waterfall. The terrain is uneven and menacing in the gloom. The thrashing sound of water pummelling against the rocks in the near distance, an ominous reminder of the dangers lurking below.

Trudging forward with caution, we reach the base without mishap, and I breathe a sigh of relief.

Julius jumps straight into action and uses his Propensity skills to raise a plume of water. "The temperature is raising rapidly. At this rate, it will reach boiling point within three days," he delivers.

"I can feel the disturbance beneath the surface. We are going to have to act quickly," agrees Thea.

Bright, flashing headlights appear above us. A night tour bus has arrived, and a guide is unloading people to take in the sights. The whole attraction is now lit up with floodlights. Alexandraya and Roman respond instinctively, extinguishing their light balls and retreating from their prominent position undetected. Following their lead, the remaining group members silently move away from the water's edge, slipping out of public view.

Departing, I spy another group leaving in a different direction simultaneously. Hmm, *strange*.

"Time to return to the apartments. We will resume tomorrow evening," directs Alexandraya.

******

A relentless tapping at the door disturbs my unexpected slumber. The travel lag crept in the moment I returned to the apartment, forcing my body to recharge despite my wish to remain alert. I had hoped to unpack the revelations Ms M delivered earlier at the Marketplace, but drifted into a dreamless sleep before I had the chance.

"Are you in there Siriarna? It's me... Roman," I hear from outside my room.

"Hang on a sec."

I open the door looking dishevelled, my hair a wayward

mess.

"Were you sleeping?"

"Well, I was trying to," I laugh.

He hurls himself onto my bed in two strides, the mattress creaking under his lanky weight. Making himself comfortable, he pats the spot beside him beckoning me over. I slide into position while discreetly attempting to flatten my hair. I must look a wreck compared to the perfectly styled Alexandraya.

"What did you get up to today? You know, before we went to the falls," he asks.

I toy with the idea of sharing Ms M's theory on my ability, but the warning from Simeon rings in my ears. I know I can trust Roman, and I don't want to lie to him, but for some inexplicable reason, I hold back the information. "I went to the Marketplace to explore." Technically, not a lie, just a withholding of information.

"Find anything interesting?"

"Lot's actually," I reply, my bangs falling into my eyes.

He reaches over and brushes the strands from my face, tucking them behind my ear. "Glad you're enjoying the realm. I can't wait to start the mission. I'm ready." He speaks confidently.

My breath catches at his touch. "I'm ready too." I exhale, although I'm not referring to the mission. Before I have the chance to elaborate, a mirrored orb appears in Roman's hand.

"Where are you, Roman?" a voice roars.

Alexandraya! She has a habit of interrupting at the most inappropriate times. I make a groaning sound that I thought was in my head but must have escaped out loud. *Did I do that on purpose? Yes, I suppose I did.*

"Is that Siriarna next to you? Are you in *her* room?" she accuses, evidently overhearing my not-so-accidental groan.

Roman jumps off my bed and rushes from my room, mouthing a wordless goodbye. Through my now closed door, I remain privy to Alexandraya's screeching tones. And my lips make an involuntary curl upwards.

CHAPTER 11

Siriarna

Winter Solstice has arrived. And, the time has come for our group to perform the mission we were sent to this realm to complete. As midnight strikes, we embark upon our journey to the power station, the remaining communication vials around our necks. Roman gives my hand a quick squeeze before joining Alexandraya at the head of the group to light our way.

We follow the same protocol used the last time we were here—through the power station to the maintenance shaft and to the tunnel that leads directly to the base of the falls. This time, I have no hesitation climbing down the ladder. *Thank you, Braxton.*

As a precautionary measure, Leister and Sage remain positioned at the top of the waterfall to circumvent any possible arising issues. On cue, a mirrored orb appears in Alexandraya's hand and Leister confirms the area is clear.

"Okay, let's get this done," says Alexandraya brimming with positive enthusiasm.

Julius moves forward, chants, and points his blue-stained finger to the cascading waterfall stopping the mighty flow mid-stream. Then he and Brooklyn raise the entire watery contents of the whirlpool above the earth. It is impressive to see how far their powers have come since the Propensity Selections.

Alexandraya tries to use a light shard to slice open the earth and tunnel it toward the core. However, it does not penetrate the exposed exterior.

"We can't hold this volume of water much longer," utters Julius in a deeply strained voice.

"I'll slow down Time as much as I can without stopping it," Braxton says, jumping in with a chant. Ribbons of Time appear in his left palm. He selects the string relating to the Surface Word and expertly twists it between his right thumb and fingers.

"Help me Roman," Alexandraya says urgently.

"If I do that Alexandraya, we will lose all light, and no one will be able to see a thing."

I throw a suggestion into the conversation, "What if we use an electrical current to try and create a fault line?"

Alexandraya's eyes narrow into slits, her lips purse and she shoots a hostile glare in my direction. But she knows this is a good idea and soon concedes. "Mykos should be the one to do it. His skills are far superior to yours Siriarna and we can't take the chance that you won't stuff it up. This is not a classroom experiment."

Without hesitation and with his chest puffed out from Alexandraya's praise, Mykos steps forward. He chants and points his purple finger at the ground under the suspended water. It doesn't work. He tries again but, still, he cannot penetrate the stubborn ground. "I think I see movement," he says optimistically.

Yeah, I don't think so.

"Hey Siriarna, I think you should try," pipes up Roman, making eye contact and giving me his standard wink.

I'm questioning if his faith in me is severely misplaced. But after the one-on-one time we shared in my room, I need to show him I can do it. For my own pride.

Mykos glares at me, eyes narrowed with haughty scepticism. The doubt creeps in.

"Guys. Seriously. We can't hold this water much longer." Julius says, straining under the enormous pressure.

Brooklyn's eyes are closed while she concentrates all her Propensity strength on the task. The sweat dripping down her forehead, the only giveaway of her struggle.

"Give it a try Siriarna, work with Mykos and create the fault line." Roman encourages.

"Are you insane Roman? She is as useless as mortal right now. Everything she does is sub-standard. She can barely use her skills. She's only here because Simeon felt sorry for her. She should never have been part of this mission." Alexandraya spits out the words with pure hatred.

At the insult, a flash of anger burns behind my eyes, begging to be released. Way too pent up to try and rein in the building force, I direct my gaze to the location where Alexandraya is unsuccessfully working her light shard. A crack immediately appears. Slow at first but gathering momentum, catapulting its way directly to the Earth's centre.

"I did it," rejoices Alexandraya, hugging her body in self-congratulation.

I'm dumbfounded. Does she really think *she* opened the fault line? Seriously? But from the way she is gloating, it's obvious she does. I did not use a chant nor point my finger to the split point. I used my mind, and no one witnessed it.

As soon as the crack reaches the core, the problem is exposed. A blindingly bright, gooey liquid is slowly leaking and rising, heading straight for the surface. Henry steps forward using his magic to shroud the liquid with a shot of darkness, enough so we can comfortably see the issue.

"Thea, Rebecka, it's time to use your Earth alchemical powers and stop this leak," Alexandraya directs with her newfound power confidence.

Both girls simultaneously chant and circle their green Propensity fingers. A covalent chemical bond appears, hovering above the exposed earth. Together they work in unison, suspending the magical elixir before carefully wielding it into position.

I am holding my breath at the complexity of this critical element. It will determine if we succeed in our debut Surface World mission. The stakes have never been higher.

Eyes locked together, Thea slowly nods her head to Rebecka, and both girls release the elixir. The heat of the chemical bond hisses as it encounters the escaping molten. Within seconds, the cavity is successfully sealed. The bleeding heart of the earth is now healed. And my breathing returns to normal.

Suspended water crashes down refilling the whirlpool, and the waterfall returns to its previous flowing glory. Brooklyn drops to her knees and weeps at the relief of releasing her power. Julius crouches beside her taking her hand in his. They are bound by the enormity of this momentous experience.

Emotions are running high. I turn and outstretch my arms ready to congratulate the semi god next to me. It's Alexandraya. She physically recoils at my gesture, turning to Roman instead. Henry fills the gap left behind and shakes my hand in congratulation.

There will be no sign of any interference. And no mortal will ever be aware of how an underlying disaster, almost struck their realm.

The sun is starting to rise but Henry intervenes and

covers it with darkness. "Time for some well-deserved rest guys, this will give us a few hours," he says as we wander back to the apartments for the last time.

As we leave, I notice the same stealth group from the other evening vanish behind the waterfall. *The Core?*

CHAPTER 12

Siriarna

After a successful mission, a chariot is summoned to return us to Evolirium. Surreptitiously we climb aboard, shielded from exposure by a veil of glamour. The chatter amongst the group is subdued compared to our initial mission departure as exhaustion sets in, each semi god lost in their own thoughts.

Back on Evolirium, we make our way to the dormitory huts to catch up on some much-needed rest. It's also a good chance to combat the travel lag before tomorrow's debriefing with High Power Omnisensus. I hang back, happy to walk on in silence. Taking my time, I stop in the meadows, find a patch of clover, lie back, and close my eyes while breathing in the lightly scented Evolirium air.

"Hey, Siriarna, mind if I join you?"

Opening my eyes, I spy Braxton's floppy chestnut hair. "Sure, pull up a clove."

"That was a great mission, don't you think?" he says smiling, taking a seat next to me. "I bet your guide parents will be thrilled when you tell them all about it."

"As I'm sure yours will be, too." I return his smile.

Braxton shrugs. "Maybe. I mean, my guide mother will be, but my guide father really couldn't care less."

"What was it like, living with your guide parents?" I ask cautiously, catching his voice change when speaking about his guide father.

"I couldn't wait to get out of the Home Realm. I stayed longer than I wanted because I didn't want to leave Paulette with that man. Paulette summoned a chariot for my 15th birthday. She said my life had to progress, that my future awaited. She said she'd chosen hers, with Nicholas, and she had accepted it a century ago." His eyes fill with a nostalgic mist as he speaks about Paulette.

"She seems like a wonderful guide." I gently respond.

Nodding, he says, "She is, and I should visit her more often. As soon as my powers progress, I will return to the

Home Realm and set things straight."

His jaw has set into a tight clench, and I place a comforting hand on his shoulder, "You are gifted with magic Braxton. I'm sure you will achieve everything you wish for."

"I spend as much time as I can studying every chant and Propensity history on Time. I knew in the Home Realm Time was my future. I have my sights set on The Core, then I will be able to help Paulette. And Nicholas will pay for the misery he has caused."

The passion in his voice is a mix of determination and hurt. "The Core would be lucky to have you." I say gently.

"What about you? Do you have any future plans brewing away?" he asks changing the subject.

My brow furrows as thoughts of Ms M and her revelations enter my mind space. "Hmm, not really." I say absently biting my lip.

"Siriarna, you look like you have the weight of the realm on your shoulders. Do you want to talk about it?"

I am in two minds, but the concern spread across Braxton's face counteracts Simeon's warning and I share my secret. "I had a reading by a mortal clairvoyant, and her discovery has left me with many questions."

The relief of sharing my new burden is instantaneous. Braxton is encouraging and patient, listening intently as I speak. He shows no judgement as I explain my new magic development, even when I tell him I have no control over the erratic nature of this new power. "You know, I don't think there has ever been another semi god in history with such a skill. It is usually a high god's-only power," he muses thoughtfully.

I had the same thought which is why I am so confused. My pulse begins to race, "Please can you swear to me you won't mention any of this to another soul? I don't need anyone else treating me like a freak, especially while I work out exactly what's happening to me."

"Of course, I won't. I swear," he says crossing his heart with his finger to make his point. "And Siriarna, I'm here to help if ever you need a friend to talk to or test your power on." He winks.

I laugh, "I might just take you up on that."

"Anytime."

Rubbing my eyes, the travel lag catching up with me, I yawn. "I have to sleep now, I'm completely wrecked. See you tomorrow." Standing, I add, "And Braxton, thank you."

******

Refreshed from a great night's rest in my own surroundings, I arrive at the Reading Hub early and find all other mission group members had the same idea.

Roman beckons to me. He has saved a space next to him on the couch. I gladly accept his invitation and slide into the empty space. "Isn't it great being back on Evolirium a hero?" he says as I fold into the space beside him.

"Yeah, it's pretty great," I say, flashing my widest grin.

Successfully fulfilling our fated life purpose is like an addictive drug to semi gods. The magical endorphins released, leaves behind a craving for more. It's a revolving exhilarating lifecycle. And one built into our DNA by the Fates.

Alexandraya flinches when I take my seat on the other side of Roman, and her eyes narrow to slits when she observes my smile. "It's a bit tight now you're here Siriarna. Care to change couches so we can spread out a bit? I'm getting claustrophobic vibes," she smiles tightly.

Before I have a chance to rise and relocate, High Power

Omnisensus enters the chamber and starts his speech, "I am tremendously proud of the outstanding job you all performed during this mission. And your efforts have been noticed by the gods themselves."

"It has indeed," calls a distant and approaching voice.

A great flash of golden light envelopes the room and Hermes himself is now standing in front of us, arriving by winged helmet and winged sandals. Twelve shocked and astounded faces suck in a sharp breath of air at the same time. It is extremely rare for a great god to enter the Progression Realm. This is a huge honour.

Hermes continues... "We have been keeping a close eye on the way this group handled the mission. It was a difficult task for your first foray into the Surface World as a servant of the Fates and protector of humanity. You did your Realm and Leaders proud. And in doing so, you have saved hundreds of thousands of lives and stopped catastrophic damages. Your training has served you well."

One person interrupts the great god's speech. "Thank you, Your Greatness. I oversaw this mission and believe the strong leadership was the reason for our success. In fact, it was I who parted the Earth's crust, allowing the repair to take place."

Alexandraya.

Are there no limits to her outspokenness? Besides, she's wrong, she didn't part the crust. I want so desperately to set the record straight, but I catch Braxton's eye and he shakes his head.

Hermes flashes a smile in her direction, "You should be most proud. I will be keeping my eyes on all of you," he announces; however, his gaze is focussed solely on Alexandraya.

Discussion over, Hermes leaves the chamber and Evolirium in a remarkable disappearing flash of golden light.

Wrapping up the debriefing, High Power Omnisensus says, "What an unexpected and excellent surprise. To have acknowledgement from Hermes is superlative. You may all return to your Propensities," he beams before dismissing the group.

Alexandraya pushes past me, leaving the chamber without a backward glance, head held high.

She is going to be more insufferable than normal.

"Is she for real?" Braxton whispers in my ear as he passes.

I giggle. I'm really starting to like this guy.

******

Alexandraya

Hermes' arrival here on Evolirium is more than I could have hoped for. He is as glorious as the images I had pictured in my dreams, with his strong build and smooth chiselled jawline. So very good looking in his eternal youth. And his arrival by golden winged sandals and helmet—well, that was just plain extraordinary.

Speaking to him directly was every bit as exciting as I had expected. The glint in his eyes when he looked me up and down was exactly what I'd hoped for. Even for a great god, he is not immune to my appearance. And he is perfectly welcome to look.

Goddess Alexandraya. I start imaging our wedding. Perhaps I am a bit ahead of myself, but there is no harm in dreaming. After all, dreams can come true, and I will be doing everything in my well-practiced power to ensure mine do exactly that.

******

Siriarna

Following the debriefing, I make my way back to the Electricity Propensity classroom. Mykos is casually slouching on a desk in the centre of the room when I arrive. He is animatedly retelling stories of our mission to the huddled members of our group. I walk over to join the discussion, but Astrid and Eloise close the gap, freezing me out.

I hoped Mykos would help smooth things over with the group by including me in his retelling. But he obviously has no intention of doing so; even though I *was* the right choice for this mission, proven when I successfully penetrated the Earth when he couldn't.

Me, Me, Me, I think with growing anger.

The lights start to flicker. *Oh no, it's happening again.* My pulse is racing, heat is rushing to my cheeks and my eyes are a burning fire of rage. Eloise lets out an ear-piercing scream as broken glass shatters like a tornado around the room. Everyone dives under nearby desks to protect themselves from the falling debris. Everyone but me.

Simeon witnesses the event from the classroom

doorway. He rushes toward me and whisks me away from the fallout.

"Stay here," he instructs. "I'll be back in a moment."

From the hallway, I hear him dismiss the class, blaming the incident on faulty electrical wiring. My teammates rush from the classroom, the aftereffects of the incident still fresh and concerning, unaware I am missing from the group. And unaware *I* was the cause of the catastrophe.

"I think it's time we have a little chat Siriarna," Simeon decrees as he ushers me back into the classroom.

The colour drains from my face. I can't believe the destruction I just caused. It's confronting and scary. Simeon sits at a table and indicates for me to do the same. Numbly, I do as he instructs.

"I see your powers are expanding," he starts.

"I don't understand what just happened. I wasn't trying to injure anyone," I lower my head miserably.

"We must find out what is triggering these outbreaks, and you must learn to control your power," he says.

"Okay." It's all I can manage. I'm listening, but I'm not really hearing the words Simeon is speaking.

"This is not a punishment, Siriarna. You have such great potential. It's time for us to dig a little deeper and for you to learn control. Go home now and recompose. Tomorrow is a new day. We will work together during our morning sessions and figure this out together," he says brightly, trying to comfort me.

But all I hear is 'control' and that is something I fear I am unable to manage.

Instead of going home, I head straight for Roman's hut. I need to unload the burden weighing on my mind with my best friend. Knocking on his door, I am already slightly happier. All emotion vanishes as Alexandraya opens the door.

"What are you doing here 'basic'?" she snarls.

I turn and silently retreat from the hut.

"That's right, go. We don't want you here. You're always in the way—"

I hear Alexandraya's words fading out behind me as I walk away briskly. The walk soon turns into a jog. The sweat begins to drip down my face and with each droplet, I increase my pace. I follow the pathway straight to the Zen. I'm sprinting now and the wind in my damp hair is exhilarating. It's keeping me from thinking about the obliterated light bulb in the Propensity classroom and Eloise's horrified scream.

My breathing has become ragged, my heartbeat pounding in my chest. I stop by the water fountain to drink, splash my face, and catch my breath. Then I make my way to the electrical boards. I sit in the middle and try to think about turning on the lights with my mind. Nothing. It's infuriating.

"Fancy seeing you here."

I swing my head over my shoulder and find Braxton standing behind me. Before he has a chance to sit, I blurt out the whole classroom debacle, finishing with my chat to Simeon. The relief of getting it off my chest is immediate.

Braxton patiently listens to the whole story. He suggests we go over each time I've manipulated electricity by thought to see if we can find a common link. I share with him the incidents in order and severity, but neither of us can find a connection.

"Would you like me to turn back time to before this afternoon's explosion?" He offers gallantly.

"I didn't know you were able to conjure a spell that advanced?"

"Yeah, I'm kind of working with the advanced years' students in private," he responds sheepishly.

I consider his offer, it's very tempting. But I remember his previous warnings about memory loss after a time shift. If I can't remember what I did, how can I stop it from reoccurring? Hanging my head, I decline his proposition.

I raise a hand to my temple. It's throbbing from overanalysing, and my mind needs a break.

"Are you okay?" Braxton asks watching my movement. "Perhaps we should go. I'll walk you home," he offers.

A lone butterfly hovers, then flutters beside me the entire journey home. It gives me a sense of comfort and, strangely, my headache disappears.

CHAPTER 13

Siriarna

There is no physical damage to be seen. Our Propensity classroom has been completely cleaned, banishing any evidence of broken glass. I wish I could just as easily scrub the memory from my mind, however, there seems to be no hint of unrest from the other group members. At least that is some small consolation.

Letting out a deep-seated sigh as I sink into my self-designated chair at the back of the classroom, I try to focus on my breathing in the hope of mentally relaxing.

Simeon storms through the doorway, snapping my attention away from my breathing exercises. He strides purposefully to the front of the classroom where he then unravels a scroll. Clearing his throat dramatically he begins to read, announcing the much-anticipated third quarter Challenge to the class.

> "Upon the 100th moment on the 7th day;
>
> The annual Challenge comes your way;
>
> Teams of two should follow each clue;
>
> But take your time to think them through;
>
> Work together, find the guise;
>
> Use your skills, and partner wise;
>
> This will be your ultimate test;
>
> And lead to this year's true and best."

This is exactly the distraction I needed. Although, I can't help but wonder if my magic will behave.

Excited chatter fills the room. The others seem to forget my exile and include me in their conversations.

"Isn't this the most exciting thing to happen?" says Astrid with glee.

Frasier's face spreads into a widened grin, "I'm pretty pumped. It won't be long until we graduate and become Second Years."

"Do you think we can partner with anyone from any

Propensity? The riddle is kind of vague," adds in Eloise.

"We only have five members, and it says, "partner wise," so I'm guessing we can, or else there will be one person from our Prop going solo," I cautiously join in.

"Ooh, that's a great point, Siriarna. I think you might be right," Astrid nods her head in agreement.

"We are stronger together. I think you and I should work together, Astrid," suggests Eloise.

"Yes, I agree with Eloise. Let's pair up Frasier," remarks Mykos.

Now, with my four peers paired up, I am once again, the odd one out.

"Sorry, Siriarna. I'm not trying to be mean. I am just more connected with Astrid," says Eloise.

"Don't worry about it," I respond casually.

It does leave the question of who I should partner with. Or more to the point, who would want to partner with me. Normally, Roman would be my go-to but with Alexandraya in the picture, that rules him out. My mind wanders to Braxton.

"Right, all. There is still work to be done. Take your seats," Simeon interrupts the banter.

I can't concentrate because I am thinking about how

to approach Braxton. On a positive note, I've stopped worrying about shattering the new classroom lighting.

The end of class bell blasts indicating mid-break and my nerves return as I ready my search for Braxton.

I see Roman sitting with the TON and give him a small wave of acknowledgement, which he returns. His three companions do not. I head to the top of the grassy mounds, where I have a good vantage over all the groups scattered around the Zen. I can't see Braxton. He normally sits by the river with the Sixth Year Time Propensity students, but he is not there now. I start to lose my nerve and plonk myself down where I'm standing.

"Hi, Siriarna. How are you feeling today?" Braxton asks sitting down beside me.

"Much better thank you. Um, did your Group Leader announce the third quarter Challenge this morning?" I ask, plucking a blade of grass from the soil and twisting it between my fingers.

"Yes, she did."

"Oh, um, good." *What is wrong with me? Ask now.*

"I can't wait to participate. Group Leader Gisella told our class the final clue was thought up by the Sixth Year students," he discloses, clearly impressed.

Now is the perfect opportunity to ask him to be my partner. I want to, I really do but my throat constricts, and my mouth is suddenly dry. I can't seem to find the words. Instead, I just stare at him. *I must look like an absolute idiot.*

"Are you okay there, you look a bit pale?"

It's time, I'm going to do it... "I was wondering if you might, maybe, if you haven't already got someone else in mind, perhaps, consider being my partner in the Challenge?" I somehow manage to get the way-too-many words out. I lift my head and see the corners of Braxton's mouth turn upwards.

"I was hoping you were going to ask me. And the answer is 'yes'," he grins.

Relief floods through me. *That wasn't so hard!*

"Let the 7-day countdown begin," he declares before we head back to our respective classes in opposite directions.

I hear a voice from behind calling out my name. I spin around and see Roman following me on the pathway, jogging to catch up. "I think we should partner up in the challenge," he says matter-of-factly when he reaches me.

"I thought you'd be teaming up with Alexandraya."

"I know she wants to partner with me, but I wanted to do this with you, Siriarna. Like old times," he asks hopefully.

"I would have liked nothing more Roman, only I just asked Braxton to be my partner and he accepted."

"*You* asked him." His expression is unconvinced. "That doesn't sound like something you would normally do."

"Well, things are changing Roman. I'm changing."

With a frown, he says, "I'm starting to see that."

We continue walking the rest of the way to our classrooms in silence. Before I enter mine, Roman asks if he can walk me home. "Just like old times," he adds.

However, when class finishes a few hours later, he is nowhere to be seen. Disappointed, I start my solo journey home, stopping in the meadow to gather my thoughts. I can't help but wonder why Roman stood me up, especially as walking home together was his suggestion. It seems I'm not the only one who has changed.

A kaleidoscope of butterflies surrounds me, some land on my shoulder, others my face. The flutter of their wings tickles my skin and drags the grey from my mood.

When I arrive home an hour later, Roman is leaning

against my front door. "Sorry, Siriarna, I finished class early and had some errands to run," he explains.

He looks flushed and coy. Years of friendship tell me he's lying. For a moment I wonder where he has really been, but I see his shirt is misbuttoned and the answer is clear—Alexandraya.

"Don't worry about it. We can catch up another time." I say mustering up as much nonchalance as I can.

"I wanted to see you. Can I come in?"

"Sure," I smile. Internally, I am seething at my weakness in not being able to send him on his way.

He launches himself onto my couch and stretches out his long limbs, making himself completely at home. I join him, although I am a lot less relaxed.

Casually, folding his arms behind his head, he gets straight to the point. "So, I am here to convince you to dump Braxton and join me in the challenge."

I wasn't sure why he was so intent on seeing me today, but this I did not see coming. "I can't do that Roman. It's not the right thing to do."

"Sure, you can. Friends First Always," he winks.

It's a low blow using our mantra to try and change my decision, but I stand firm.

"I don't understand why you're so desperate to be my partner in the Challenge. I've barely seen you since you started dating Alexandraya."

"That's exactly *why* we should do this together."

My jaw clenches, "I won't do it Roman. Sorry."

"Have it your way then."

He stands without making eye contact and exits my hut in two strides, slamming the door behind him.

CHAPTER 14

Siriarna

I can't believe how swiftly the week went by; I've barely had time to think. And now, the much anticipated third quarter Challenge is here. A flutter of nerves tingles inside my stomach at the prospect of competing against so many talented students.

The Auditorium is a rainbow of colour as all students arrive wearing their Propensity uniforms. The atmosphere is electric, which is doing nothing to calm my nerves.

Winning the Challenge is the year's greatest honour and with it, comes the greatest reward. The victors will have their names etched in the Grand Auditorium Hall of

Fame and will travel to Mount Olympus to dine with a table of Gods. They will also lead the next Surface World mission. There is no doubt that the competition will be ruthless because this is a prize worth fighting for.

Group Leaders, together with High Power Omnisensus, are positioned on the platform at the front of the room. They stand behind a long table holding the clue scrolls for each team. I spy a nod between them before I hear the horn blast.

"Commence," the Authority announces to the chaotic room.

The Challenge has begun with a flurry of activity. Teams run to the table to grab their first clue. Davina and Melodie push past me, sneering in sync, "move 'basic'."

Alexandraya and Roman are close behind. Roman looks at me with a sheepish expression.

Alexandraya laughs, "Ah, Siriarna, you don't need to rush, it's not like you've even got a chance to win this."

Turning my back, I start searching for Braxton. He isn't as easy to spot because he isn't as tall as Roman. I scan the rapidly emptying room and spy him at the side of the hall, looking in my direction.

"There you are," he says as I approach.

"Let's do this," I say with a newfound confidence. The TON's dismissal has me psyched up, and I am going to give this challenge a red-hot crack. I want to win. *So damn badly.*

We are the last team to collect our clue scrolls. High Power Omnisensus gives me a knowing little nod and Simeon grins, winking at me when I collect mine. *Hmm, strange.*

I return to Braxton and unravel our scroll. It reads:

> Take your time, but use haste;
> Use each clue, but do not waste;
> Look forward, see behind;
> Use your skills, they're one of a kind.

Braxton scratches his head and looks at me quizzically. We are the only people remaining in the Auditorium. Everyone else has bolted out the double doors keen to solve the riddle and find their next clue. Instead of following the other teams and the mayhem that followed, I read the rhyme out loud in the now quietened space. "Let's break down the clue." I say methodically.

"We've definitely taken our time. Maybe we can use

some haste when we find the next clue." Braxton says repeating line two.

It's a good thought so I concentrate on the third line. I wonder how we can look forward from behind. I turn my head to look over my shoulder but nothing significant stands out. As I spin around to face Braxton, I spot an object near the entrance—the gilded mirror with the 6 Propensities carved into the oversized frame. "Come on partner." I smile.

"Where are we going?"

"You'll see." I giggle at the joke, dragging him toward the mirror.

Standing side by side, facing our reflections, we peer closely into the mirror. I see Braxton's eyes staring back at me intently and I shyly avert my gaze. That's the moment I spot a glint from the chalice cup. Without a word, I grab Braxton's hand and race to the front of the Auditorium. Reaching inside the cup, I pull out a slip of paper. Bingo! Clue 2.

"Gods likely Siriarna, you are so clever," Braxton hugs me, and together, we unfold the piece of paper. It reads:

Good for you, you've found Clue 2;

But now the race picks up its pace;

There is no time for you to waste;

Follow the track to where it leads;

It's quite a way so use your speed;

It could be solid or maybe hollow;

Get right to it, it's time to follow.

"The Ovallium Forest" we say in unison. I cover my mouth, shocked by the volume that escaped in excitement.

"Let's go," Braxton whispers, zipping the second clue into his backpack.

Alexandraya, Roman, Melodie and Davina appear out of nowhere. I can't help giving Alexandraya the biggest smile I can summon as I walk through the double doors.

******

Alexandraya

I catch that sarcastic grin from Siriarna. Perhaps I hadn't given her enough credit to rate her as a possible threat in this challenge. Really, her skills are so average, but I had not given any thought to her mind. All those books she reads might actually give her an advantage. I was hoping she would be derailed with Roman by my side, however, she seems rather unaffected.

A rush of anger bolts through my body. This challenge is mine and I have every intention of winning. I don't care about the winner's inscription in the Auditorium (although it would be nice to see my name every time I enter). I don't even care so much about the next Surface World mission (again, I wouldn't mind leading it). What I really care about is the dinner with the gods and another chance to meet Hermes.

Winning this challenge is everything. I will make sure I end up on top. Whatever it takes.

******

Siriarna

Braxton and I are hustling along the pathway. We pass through the Zen, but we still have a way to go and need to get to the dock quickly. The boat will take us directly to the edge of the forest. Out of nowhere, my hair swishes into my face. I can narrowly make out the four figures leaving a channel of light behind. The TON, and Roman, have used their Light speed to race ahead.

By the time Braxton and I arrive, the forest appears deserted. The fresh smell of pine needles and damp moss fills my nostrils. The leaves are crunching below my feet and the dappled light is fading as the forest thickens the further we plough. I can't hear any voices or view signs of other teams.

Taking a moment, Braxton reaches into his backpack and hands me a bottle of stream water.

"You have thought of everything," I say gulping down the cool liquid.

"Well, I try."

The moment he says it, we both look at each other and say out loud, "the old well."

The old well is located East past the centre point of the forest. We change our direction and set about the new course. Once we arrive, we see another team leaving, Sage and Brooklyn.

Positioned across the top of the well, tied to a broken winch, is the end of a piece of rope. I peak over the mossy stone wall, but see only darkness. At first glance, there is no way to estimate its depth. Braxton fetches a rock and tosses it over the side of the well and we wait for a sound to indicate the bottom. Minutes pass and after what seems like an eternity, we hear a resounding splash from the abyss.

"This pit seems fathomless. It will take hours to pull the rope up by hand, even if we take turns. Any brilliant ideas on how we can raise the bucket?" I ask.

"Not yet. The well refers to the 'hollow' line of the clue. I'm guessing we should now search for something solid," he replies whilst kicking the surrounding dirt and raising a pile of dust. The movement catches a stone that ricochets off his shoe and into the side of the cobbled well. "That's it. We'll use a large boulder and tie the end of the rope to it, then lower it. That should catapult the bucket to the top much faster than we could manually pull it," he figures.

"Brilliant. Great thinking Braxton."

Moving back through the thicket, we manage to locate a decent sized boulder. It takes our combined strength to roll it toward the well. Sweating and dusty, Braxton unties the rope from the winch and secures it around the stone's girth. I fuse the end of the knot together with a zap of electricity and together we raise the boulder to the side of the well. Then, with a mighty shove, we launch it over the edge. Braxton was right, the bucket flies to the surface within seconds. I plunge my hand into the bottom of the bucket and take out our third clue.

I hug him in congratulations "Great job partner. Who knew this challenge would be so dirty?" I laugh looking down at my now grey streaked training shirt. "But seriously, do you think we'll catch the other teams? There's got to be at least three in front of us now," I add earnestly.

"Don't fret my lady, we have all the time in the world." He chants and the ribbons of Time appear in his palm.

"I'm guessing you reversed time?" I laugh noticing the bucket is no longer hanging from the winch. I don't think I'll ever get used to the feeling of something missing and not knowing quite what it might be.

"Indeed, I did." Braxton says handing me the third clue.

It reads:

Well, look and see, here's clue 3;
You're halfway there;

So, don't despair;
About your position in this race;
You may come 1st, 2nd or even last place;
Don't give up, keep on searching;
The winners will be truly deserving.

A crunching sound followed by voices can be heard in the distance, indicating another team is right behind us.

"Shhh," Braxton whispers, finger over his lips.

Nodding my agreement, we move without a backward glance, silently creeping undetected out of the Ovallium Forest.

We find Sage and Brooklyn sitting beside the concrete pathway on the grass with their heads bent. They are studying the latest clue. Braxton and I nod toward them and continue moving forward. Both girls stand and trail behind.

"Looks like we have company," Braxton lowers his voice. "I think, they think, we know where we're going."

"Don't we?" I chuckle.

Jumping on a boat to catch our breath and conserve some energy, we find a space to rest and scan over the third clue. From the corner of my eye, I spy Sage and Brooklyn follow and sit behind us. Braxton folds the clue and pops it into his backpack.

The boat docks by the meadows and we exit, the girls keeping a close distance. I stop abruptly and scratch my head.

"Do you guys know where you're going or not?" Sage asks impatiently as she reaches our standstill.

"Not." Braxton responds innocently.

"For gods' sake, we've wasted our time following these two." Brooklyn adds before taking Sage's hand and retreating in a huff, leaving us alone.

"Now they're gone, let's figure out this clue," Braxton suggests, sitting on a patch of soft clover covered earth.

I sit next to him and lean in closely to read the riddle. Braxton flinches at our new proximity and my face flushes in response. I reread the same line over and over, even though I know them by heart. One word seems misplaced. "Why do you think the clue calls the Challenge a race? It's not just about speed." I ask somewhat preoccupied.

"That's it, Siriarna, you've nailed it! The clue must be hidden somewhere in the sportsground." Braxton says jumping to his feet with fresh enthusiasm.

Reaching down, he pulls me to my feet. We're standing face to face now, eyes meeting. Pulse racing, I pull my gaze away and glance over my shoulder, making sure there are no teams lurking nearby. "We're good to go," I say staring at the meadow's sleeping flowers.

"Oh, ah, good."

We move briskly, but my steps cannot keep up with my racing heartbeat.

Past the Learning Facility we traipse until we arrive at the adjacent sports fields. Two teams are already on the fields surveying the perimeter. Braxton tells me he thinks the clue will be at the finish line on the circular track. It's a good thought, but I don't see how a clue could be hidden in the open space. Still, we move toward the line, search the track, but do not find a clue. This is getting frustrating. My fellow Propensity members, Astrid and Eloise, have now joined us at the line.

"Wanna work together on this one?" Eloise suggests.

"Yeah, good idea," I agree and read the clue out loud to the four of us.

"It *has* to be here at the finish line. That's all that makes sense," says Astrid.

Braxton nods his agreement. "Let's spread out."

The four of us stretch across the marked finish line, me closest to the grassed centre of the oval. I bend down to remove a stone from my shoe, and see flagpole holes punched into the ground. When standing, they were camouflaged by blades of grass, but my lowered position exposes their concealment. Immediately, I know I've found the right location. A smile spreads across my face.

Bending down, I take two clues from the hole. I pass one to Eloise and the other to Braxton. Another team is rushing to our location after witnessing the last clue's hiding place. The stakes are high, and the race is heating up as every team scrambles to claim victory.

"Thanks, Siriarna," the girls intone, accepting the clue.

Amicably we separate, ready to continue the challenge in our own team of two. Before they leave, Eloise informs us that Roman, Alexandraya, Melodie and Davina were all heading out of the field gate when they arrived. That confirms at least two teams are ahead of us.

Braxton watches my expression change and drapes an arm around my shoulder. "Don't worry. We're still in this. Finding the guise won't be easy. I have complete faith in us, we can still win this," he says positively.

We open the last clue:

Can you solve the final riddle?

Start by meeting in the middle;

Use the clues to connect;

Take one step back and reflect;

The final guise is rather bright;

And is hidden in plain sight.

"The middle has to be the Zen," I say to Braxton who nods his head in agreement.

"Any idea about the rest of the riddle?"

"None at all—yet."

On our way through the gate, another three teams enter the sports fields. This race is getting closer with every passing minute.

Once in the Zen, I see Roman, Alexandraya, Melodie, Davina, Brooklyn, and Sage all scattered around the space at various sites. Braxton and I sit away from the other teams on the dock, near the river.

With my feet dangling in the crystal clear water, I study the last clue. Nothing immediately pops to my mind. Taking a break, I peer into the river. The reflection staring back at me isn't blank. Flipping the clue over in my hand,

I spy a faint black mark inscribed in the corner.

Barely able to contain my excitement, I ask Braxton to pass me the other clues. As suspected, there are faint marks on the back of each piece. I assemble them into a form that makes a pattern and summon my Propensity power, electrostatically adhering the four separate paper pieces into one big square.

"Siriarna–"

I stop Braxton mid-sentence, grab his hand, and drag him toward the light pillars.

"Hey, slow down. Where are we going?" he puffs, out of breath from the quick exertion.

"We need to hold the paper up to the light pillars. I think they will unravel these marks and lead us to the guise."

"Oh my gods, you're right."

Skin tingling and faces flushed, we run to the pillars. In our haste, we fail to see Roman and Alexandraya's eyes following our every move.

Standing beside the pillars, we take one step back per the fourth line of the last clue.

As I hold up the now fused square, light refracts from the pillars through the paper in a wave like motion. It deepens the faint black marks, unveiling a completed symbol.

"I know this Braxton! It's the gods' symbol for knowledge. The guise is in the Knowledge Room." I announce with barely controlled hysteria. My heart is palpitating at twice its normal speed, my body shaking with excitement at the discovery.

Though my elation is soon replaced with horror as Alexandraya appears beside me. "Thanks for working that one out, Siriarna. All's fair in love and war–not so much for you though. Now, off to claim my win."

She clenches Roman's hand and speeds off, knocking me to the ground in the process. I did spy a sympathetic look from Roman, but he didn't stop.

"Are you ok, Siriarna?" Braxton bends down, giving me his hand.

I'm not physically hurt, more pride wounded.

"I can't stand the fact the Alexandraya is going to win because she cheated." I say as he pulls me to my feet.

"Don't worry, she still has to find the guise."

"Oh, I'm not giving up. I've more fight left."

He raises a brow, "Well, let's get going."

We might not have arrived at the Knowledge Room as

quickly as Alexandraya and Roman, but I know this place better than my home hut.

Walking through the doors, I bump straight into Roman who's looking frantically around the room.

"I'm so sorry, Siriarna," he says on approach.

"Apology not accepted," I respond through clenched teeth.

"It's just–"

Cutting him off, I spit, "I don't know what's happened to you Roman, but I will not let her get away with this. I promise you." With the words spewed out, I spin around and stalk off in the opposite direction.

Upon witnessing the exchange, Braxton suggests I take a moment to calm my thoughts. Agreeing, I follow him down the spiral staircase into the Reading Hub.

The exchange with Roman has unsettled me. My thoughts are blinded with anger, and for a few minutes, we are plunged into darkness.

Me?

The transition between darkness to light causes my eyes to blink at the adjustment. Instead of closing my eyes to refocus, I open them wider, letting the light dilate my pupils. As I do, an image floats behind my lenses.

Concentrating, I try to project it forward. For a few seconds, a symbol materialises before vanishing.

The vision has cost me my balance, and I plummet toward the floor. Braxton reacts quickly catching my head before it smashes into the ground.

"Whoa, Siriarna. What just happened?"

"I know where to find the guise! The light adjustment triggered a vision. Braxton, it was amazing."

And a little bizarre if I'm honest.

"It must have been, it knocked you off your feet. Are you hurt?"

"I'm fine and I'll be even better once we win this challenge. We're looking for a book with a spine of gold marked with Athena's symbol."

"Of course, that makes perfect sense—knowledge in the Knowledge Room. I know exactly where to look, c'mon." Braxton says shooting up the stairs, two at a time.

I smack straight into Davina as I reach the top.

"What are *you* smiling at Basic?" she sniggers.

"Nothing." I meet her eyes and continue to follow Braxton.

Both girls pivot and follow me. There's not much I can do to dissuade them; we will simply have to find the book first. Braxton moves through the crescent shaped bookshelves until we reach the westernmost point of the Knowledge Room. There we find the book section marked philosophy, and I join him at his side. Melodie and Davina stand behind, waiting to pounce. Rows of shelves reveal black spined books, nothing in gold—they all look the same. Maybe I'm wrong and the vision I had meant nothing.

"They've no idea where it is. Useless as usual. Let's go." Melodie says to Davina, whose eyes bore into mine as she departs.

Braxton slides his hand into mine and gives it a light squeeze. "Are you okay?"

"I know it's here. I *feel* it."

Spying the window above the shelves, I move to position myself directly below it. My eyes follow the trail of light it casts on the bookshelf and from my vantage point, one book spine shines in gold, and its symbol is now prominent.

"I see it Braxton." I say, my voice wobbling.

"Go for it Siriarna, you deserve this," he replies full of encouragement.

Tentatively and with trembling hands, I pull the

volume from the shelf and open it. Out flies a holographic owl, identical to the one depicted on the book spine. After scanning our faces, it hoots, "Siriarna and Braxton are the winners. Meet in the Auditorium immediately." The owl flies through the Knowledge Room and out the window, continuing its enchanted message throughout all Evolirium.

"I can't believe we did it." I whisper to Braxton. The enormity of our win slowly sinking in.

His face is spread into a wide grin that lights up his entire face. It suits him. "I'm not one bit surprised, my lady."

Our victory is interrupted by a scream, "No, no, NO," coming from inside the Knowledge Room. Following the screech, I find Alexandraya collapsed on the floor in fits of angst and frustration. I step over her, repeating her previous words, "All's fair in love and war," and continue to the Auditorium.

That felt way too good.

******

Alexandraya

I hate her. I hate her more than I ever have. How *dare* Basic Siriarna steal this challenge from me! It was my destiny. My time to shine. Mine. I will make sure that useless little nobody is sorry. Who does she think she is, messing with me? I rule this realm. Me. Not her. She will pay for this!

******

CHAPTER 15

Siriarna

High Power Omnisensus and the six Propensity Leaders are standing at the front of the Auditorium, waiting. They approach Braxton and I as we enter, offering spirited congratulations. In all honesty, I'm in a complete state of shock. The last Leader to come forward is Simeon, "I knew you could do it, Siriarna. I'm so proud of you."

Gisella, Braxton's Propensity Leader, sends him a salute. It is a great honour for a Leader to have one of their students win the annual challenge.

The remaining students start to spill into the Auditorium. They circle around Braxton and me, each keen to congratulate us on our win. I feel like I'm floating on a cloud, and it is surreal. It is, without a doubt, the best thing that has ever happened to me on Evolirium.

Amongst all the excitement, I see Roman and the TON make their entrance. Only Roman moves in our direction. Alexandraya, Melodie and Davina remain at the back of the room.

"Well done, Siriarna. And you too Braxton," he says sincerely, at the same time looking impossibly handsome.

Beneath his smile, his face shows signs of resignation and my heart breaks a little. I follow behind as he retreats. Tapping him on the shoulder, I ask when he's facing me, "Can I talk to you for a minute?"

"Okay," he says guardedly.

"I was hoping you might swing by my hut tomorrow so we can chat?"

Before he has time to answer, Alexandraya storms over and interrupts. She gives me a curt nod, clasps Roman's hand, and reefs him from the Auditorium. I am left standing speechless.

"All students, take your seats," High Power Omnisensus announces. "It is with great pleasure that I announce this year's winners of the third quarter Challenge to be... Braxton and Siriarna."

Applause fills the room. Braxton turns to me with the biggest smile plastered across his face, and I return it with my own.

"Please join us, Siriarna and Braxton," the Authority continues.

Braxton escorts me to the platform. I feel like I should pinch myself. I can't quite believe this is happening, and to *me*.

"We mark this occasion by etching your names, along with your Propensity, into the Hall of Fame," High Power Omnisensus declares jovially.

The holographic owl flies into the Grand Auditorium and proceeds to etch our names with its beak onto the plaque before exploding into glittering iridescent light particles. The cheering from the crowd drowns out all further announcements.

This really is the best day I have ever experienced, and I don't want it to end.

After the celebrations finally conclude, Braxton escorts me home. We walk in comfortable silence, drained but elated from the day's success. At my door, I turn to thank him for being my Challenge partner and he sweeps me into a tight embrace, brushing his lips against mine.

My gasp is met with a gentle firm pressure, and I wrap my arms around his neck as I return the unexpected, but welcomed, kiss.

******

Climbing into bed, too exhausted to change out of my training uniform, I replay the day's extraordinary events before my mind fills with images of Braxton. I brush my fingers over my lips where his met mine, before drifting into a deep and contented slumber.

I do not hear the intrusion that happens around midnight.

My mouth is bound shut and my head is covered with a cloth bag. This jolts me from my sleep, and I attempt to scream and struggle. It's useless. I try to make sense of what is happening, but nothing registers. Two people are holding my body, one at my shoulders and the other has a strong grip on my ankles. I try to kick my legs, but they don't move. My head is slumped awkwardly against a torso, and I am being carried from my hut.

Panic sets in as the outside air whips against my bare arms. Whispered voices speak quickly, one person instructing the others, but they are too quiet to distinguish who they belong to. I have no choice other than to endure what is to come. What that is, I have no idea. Horrible thoughts plague my mind. I am alone and terrified.

After what seems like a hundred moments, I am awkwardly lowered into a space and dumped heavily onto the ground. It smells musty and damp. My hands and ankles are bound tightly.

Voices chant together in a spell I am unfamiliar with. The cloth covering my face is raised above my nose only, it still covers my eyes so I cannot sight my captors. As the spell completes, my head is yanked backwards, and a syrup is forced down my throat. I splutter and try to spit it out, but my mouth is forced closed, and I swallow every drop. I try to beg for mercy, but my head is dizzy. The last thing I remember is the sound of disappearing laughter before my head hits the earth and I black out.

When I wake, my head aches and my wrists hurt from their bindings. It is still dark, and I have no clue how long I have been here. Bile rises in my throat and I bend forward to throw up, the vomit catching on my head covering. Then, I start to cry. How did yesterday, the most wonderful day of my existence, turn into today's nightmare?

I can't seem to stop sobbing. My body is rigid and I'm afraid to move. Am I alone here? Is there something sinister lurking? My mind is playing tricks and exaggerating horrible possibilities of the danger that might be surrounding me. I scream at the thought. I scream until my throat is hoarse and I cry until I have no more tears to shed. The exhaustion of the action numbs my senses and I move in and out of consciousness. It's hard to know when I'm awake and when I'm dreaming.

I try to think about something else, anything but the terror inside my body. Slowing my breathing, I focus on how the surrounding darkness reminds me of the Home Realm and my guide parents' masquerade parties. At midnight, Stefanie would turn out the lights and a thousand candles would flicker in replacement, winding down the festivities to an intimate crescendo. That's when I would remove my mask, free from hiding my lacklustre magic and my wish to be someone else. Free in the darkness. Stefanie would always find me before the candles were ablaze. She would hug me and whisper how much she loved me in my ear. I dream of Linus twirling me around the dancefloor and I start to hum at the memory.

Whilst I am still terror-stricken and full of anxiety, I am certain I am alone. I fight to find a calm control, humming helps. Silencing my melody, I focus my senses on listening to my surroundings. Nothing. I hear absolutely nothing. That's how I know I'm in the Void and my panic returns with a vengeance.

Remembering the legend of the Void, the way a group of students tried to summon a great god a thousand years ago, fills me with a new horror. The students set a trap behind the Learning Facility to show off their cunning ways to the rest of their classmates. What they hadn't planned on achieving, was the capture of Zeus himself–and he was *furious*. He rose from the shackles and fired a lightning bolt at the group. Whilst it didn't strike anyone directly, the force and power of the bolt pierced the earth, creating a cavernous pit where the students fell. Zeus left the students there for weeks, injured and starving until his return. Ignoring pleas for forgiveness, he stripped their powers and banished them to The Between. He left the pit as a warning to others. A great stone wall was erected in front of the Void to discourage future students from entering the area. No one enters this part of Evolirium. *Ever.*

However, Zeus did not put me here and will not come to my rescue. *Who did put me here? And why?*

My stomach growls, a reminder I haven't eaten in days. *I'm going to rot in here.*

I start frantic rocking movements, trying to escape my bindings. Eventually I free my casting finger and I chant a spell to singe the remaining bindings, but nothing happens. I try to relax to encourage my magic to work, but it seems a useless endeavour.

"Damn you, damn you all," I scream to the empty nothingness.

CHAPTER 16

Roman

I seek out Braxton before morning classes commence. He is surprised to see me because we are not friends. I don't hate the guy, although I don't like the way he is currently spending so much time with Siriarna. Still, I don't dislike him.

"Have you seen Siriarna?" I ask him with concern.

"Not since the celebrations."

"Don't you find that a little strange? It's like she's disappeared."

"Well, we aren't in the same Propensity. I did look for her this morning, but I figured she must be caught up with her group after our win."

The way he says 'our win' grates on my nerves, but I continue with my questioning.

"At the ceremony, she invited me to her hut. I turned up last night, but her hut was empty," I continue.

"Maybe she was out with her friends and forgot all about you," Braxton returns slyly.

Is this guy for real? Siriarna would not forget about me. "Maybe you're right," I say, even though I know he's not. I move off and head straight to her Propensity room to chat with her Group Leader.

Simeon confirms he hasn't seen Siriarna since the ceremony and thought it strange she hadn't shown up yet for class. He suggests we go straight to High Power Omnisensus to express our concern.

*****

Braxton

I think Roman is right and I am worried. Very worried in fact. It's not like Siriarna to disappear. She was radiant after the win, like a light inside her had awakened a newfound confidence. I couldn't help but kiss her. And she returned it with passion. No, she wouldn't take off without a word. That I am one hundred percent sure of.

I start to worry something terrible has happened. I want so desperately to rewind time, but first year Propensity students are only skilled in manipulating up to 12 hours of Time. I, however, am able to chant a spell to rewind the full 24 hours gifted to semi gods, just like the advanced fifth and sixth year students. I pay them in gods' nectar for their secret tuition. *Thank you, Nicholas.* It's the only thing my hostile guide parent has been useful for. I wonder if he's even noticed I pilfered his stolen loot.

Even if I did rewind time, Siriarna has been missing longer than 24 hours now, so it would do no good. And, if I was caught breaking the realm rules, my time on Evolirium would be over and I would be realm-banished.

Without another thought, I head straight to High Power Omnisensus. Something is very wrong with this whole situation. When I arrive at his office, I see both Roman and Simeon sitting outside. The Authority invites us into his office, and the three of us spew words at the same time.

He raises his hands in a stop motion, "Slow down, one at a time."

Roman speaks up relaying the story of arriving at Siriarna's empty hut, and none of us having seen her since the Challenge celebration. Well, I saw her at her hut. But that is a mere technicality, and I don't want to share that private moment with Roman.

High Power Omnisensus dismisses Roman and me, explaining he will gather all Propensity Leaders and hatch out a plan to find Siriarna. While he delivers the news with steady verbiage, his eyes crinkle with concern and he tugs at his chin stubble.

Shortly after our return to class, an announcement zips around the Facility calling all students to the Auditorium. It is here that High Power Omnisensus advises Siriarna's suspected disappearance. He asks if anyone has any information on where she might be. Alexandraya raises her hand.

"Yes, Alexandraya,"

"I have no idea where Siriarna might be, although I'd guess she's likely fallen asleep somewhere with a book—it has been an exhausting few days. To help, I'd like to offer my services to attend the gods' dinner tomorrow night in her place. That is, if she hasn't shown up by then."

"Yes, that's a good idea Alexandraya considering that

you did place second in the challenge. Come to my office when we're finished here."

What?! I don't believe it. Since when has Alexandraya ever done anything helpful that's not directly self-involved? I wouldn't be surprised if she had something to do with Siriarna's disappearance.

"What have you done with Siriarna?" I pull at her arm roughly when we're dismissed.

"Hey, back off man," Roman interjects.

"I have no idea what you are talking about Braxton. If I had the slightest idea where Siriarna was, I would tell you. I don't want any bad blood between us, we will be dinner partners tomorrow night after all," she replies sweetly.

"Surely you can see she's lying, right?" I implore to Roman.

"No, she wouldn't do that," he responds, placing a protective arm around Alexandraya's shoulders.

******

Alexandraya

I can't believe tonight I will be dining on Mount Olympus. It's a dream come true. I must thank Siriarna, if she ever returns, for disappearing at the most convenient time.

I need to start preparing now so I look my best. My real goal is to capture Hermes' attention and Braxton will be easy to ditch. I can't believe my luck. This is all meant to be!

A knock at my door indicates the girls have arrived.

"Hey Alexandraya, how exciting is this?" Melodie and Davina chime together.

"I know, I'm excited beyond words. Let's work out what I'm going to wear, I need to look spectacular."

After tossing the entire contents of my wardrobe across my bed, the three of us decide on a simple black dress with spaghetti straps. It exposes my shoulders and highlights my long, jet-black hair. Simple but striking.

"Here, put this on," instructs Melodie. She passes me my signature emerald pendant, my most treasured ancestral heirloom. It matches my eyes perfectly and completes the outfit.

"Thanks girls. I believe it's time to go. I'll fill you in on all the juicy details tomorrow. But for now, my chariot awaits."

Arriving at the Zen, I find Braxton already waiting. And I must admit, he looks amazing in his tight black shirt and black jeans, his wavy hair flopping sexily over his brow. He matches my outfit perfectly, almost like we worked together. Shame his face is contorted into a scowl, it really ruins his whole look. I know he wishes I was Siriarna. Too bad, she's not here and this is my time to shine. I hope he doesn't ruin my night. I have no patience to babysit a pitiful semi god. Instead, I plan on spending my night engaging Hermes. I do hope he remembers me from our last meeting. I have such high hopes.

High Power Omnisensus is waiting at the edge of the Zen as I arrive. A cluster of students are gathered on the grassy mounds, keen to witness the realm entrance of the soon-to-arrive chariot and glimpse whichever god is at its helm. Melodie and Davina are front and centre as I knew they would be.

The Authority clasps his hands and wishes us well. Instead of graciously accepting the salutation, Braxton asks him about his plans to find Siriarna. The Authority tells us not to worry. I'm certainly not. He then assures us he will find her soon. *Hmm, we'll see.*

A great abundant stream of light blazes into the realm. Iris, Goddess of Rainbows, arrives in a chariot pulled by four snow white horses. The coloured light dances across their coats like a blank canvas. I hear a gasp from the mound where the students have gathered. The sight really is extraordinary.

Iris is tall and commanding, younger looking in person than I had expected. She exchanges short pleasantries with High Power Omnisensus and instructs us to board the chariot. She is direct and no nonsense. I like that. I board as quickly as she demands, but Braxton is dragging his feet. I give him a curt warning and he reluctantly climbs in.

At Iris' instruction, the horses take flight and we are airborne, Mount Olympus bound. I wave to the students below like a queen to her disciples. I can hardly contain my glee.

******

Braxton

Look at Alexandraya preening like a peacock. It's not right that Siriarna is not here. *Where is she?* I tried to delay this dinner, to postpone it to when she is found. But High Power Omnisensus insisted the date could not be changed. "The gods do not make exception under any circumstance," he'd said. I also tried to give my spot to someone else, I even suggested Roman. The two lovers could go together and leave me to find Siriarna myself. My pleas fell on deaf ears so here I am, climbing the ladder to board Iris' chariot. If I wasn't in the presence of a god, I would project time forward and this whole event would be over.

The journey between realms is quick and after passing through the vortex, we arrive at the golden gated entrance of the Sky Realm, at an altitude way above the mountains of Thessaly. It really is quite spectacular. But alas, even the gleaming precious metal's reflection on the horses' coats, does nothing to improve my mood.

Where Evolirium is lush and picturesque, Mount Olympus is evidentially a far superior realm. The Main Palace is surrounded by marble and covered in gold. It has an ancient richness in texture. The sheer height of the palace demands respect. My goal has been to inhabit this realm as part of The Core, and this dinner was to be my first foray toward that objective. Siriarna's disappearance has thwarted my purpose, and I loathe the way that Alexandraya has swindled her way into Siriarna's rightful place.

After descending the chariot ladder, Iris leads us past a central fountain into a dining room. She announces our presence and departs.

It's a rare honour for semi gods to be admitted to the Sky Realm. The gods pay little interest to the inhabitants of Evolirium, and our limited powers. Our purpose is to keep the peace with the Surface World, considered too demeaning for their attention, but a necessary obligation as ruled by the Fates.

Already seated at an enormous table laden with food is Athena, Artemis, Aphrodite, Ares, Hermes, and Apollo. Their presence overwhelms me and slink a few steps backward. Alexandraya, on the other hand, strides forward and takes a seat next to Hermes. She is confident, I will give her that. I notice the absence of Zeus and Hera. I was hoping to meet the Great God in person, but it seems nothing about this dinner is going to plan.

"Come and take a seat, semi god," instructs Artemis impatiently.

I do as she says and position myself next to her twin, Apollo. He seems the most approachable at the table. None of the other gods register our arrival, in fact, they look quite bored.

Iris returns with nectar and fills our glasses.

"A toast to this year's Challenge winners," Hermes cheers.

"Half of the winning team—to be correct," I say glaring directly at Alexandraya. She looks like she wants to kill me, and I'm sure she would stab me with a light shard if we weren't in the presence of greatness.

"Are there not two of you here?" asks Athena with an arched eyebrow, her curiosity piqued.

All eyes around the table turn to stare at me, and I flinch.

"Yes, Your Greatness. However, Alexandraya is sitting here in the place of my fellow Challenge winner, Siriarna, who seems to have vanished from the Progression Realm."

Chatter erupts around the table, boredom receding.

Alexandraya clears her throat and interrupts, "I offered to take the place of my dear fellow semi god so as not to delay these spectacular proceedings," she speaks sweetly in a lyrical voice.

She has caught the attention of Hermes. His gaze is focussed entirely on her, seemingly mesmerised by her beauty. Aphrodite does not look impressed.

This is my opportunity and I seize it. "Great Goddess Athena, do you think you might assist in the search for Siriarna?" I ask, shocked at my own directness.

"We do not involve ourselves in such trivial semi god issues, even if intriguing," she responds taking a sip of her nectar.

I bite the inside of my lip and my fists ball in my lap. My hackles rise when I glance at Alexandraya, who is laughing demurely while fluttering her eyelashes at something Hermes has said.

"Braxton, answer the Goddess," Alexandraya says bluntly.

Scanning the table I ask, "I'm sorry, can you repeat the question?"

When my eyes reach Aphrodite's, she holds my gaze intensely, and asks, "I asked what your Propensity specialty is."

"Time."

"You must be a very talented semi god," she says, her mouth curling into an angelic smile.

You have no idea.

Alexandraya politely excuses herself from the table. "Could someone please escort me to the powder room, I'd like to freshen up."

Hermes is quick to pull out her chair and offer his arm.

My jaw clenches—Alexandraya has waylaid my plan to leave this realm. She may have Hermes under her spell, but I am immune to her glamour. For under her veil, I see only darkness.

Time to end this charade and return to Evolirium.

CHAPTER 17

Roman

While Alexandraya and Braxton are on Mount Olympus, I start my search for Siriarna. I know High Power Omnisensus and the Propensity Leaders have organised a search party. But no one knows Siriarna like I do—we have been best friends for so long. Although, I'll admit, things have been a little tense since I started dating Alexandraya. Still, I know I'm the best person to find her.

I start at the meadow. Siriarna loves the wildflowers and roaming butterflies. In the past, we sat for hours amongst them staring at the sky, lost in thought. It is the first place she would go to gather her thoughts or chill out with one of her books. I head straight to the little rock cluster in the centre 'our spot'. She isn't there. I rack my brain to think where else she might be.

Perhaps she went into town to get supplies or buy a new outfit for the dinner she's now missing in the Sky Realm. Deep down, I know this is not really a possibility because she has been missing for too long. My chest tightens at the thought. Leaving Siriarna, after using her answer for the last clue, was not one of my finest moments. I feel guilty thinking about it. Even though it's no excuse, I wanted to win the Challenge so I could meet Zeus in person–I have recently been wondering if the rumours that he is my father are true. It's why I asked her to be my challenge partner in the first place. I know how smart she is, and I knew she would win. I was surprised and disappointed when she told me she had already asked Braxton. I can see how much he likes her and I'm not sure I'm okay with that. I know it's selfish as I am dating Alexandraya, but I don't want him to have her either.

In town, I search through every shop, café, and supply store to no avail. No one has seen her. Next, I try the mountain base where the elixir refill spout is located. Siriarna is addicted to mountain elixir. Maybe she went to replenish her supply and had an accident in the mountains. This thought causes my stomach to drop. I can't bear the thought of her lying hurt and alone.

Could it be as simple as her having lost track of time and falling asleep in the Reading Chamber? I'm sure that's the first place the search party would look. Still, I leave the mountains and make my way back to the Learning Facility. Just in case.

******

Siriarna

My teeth start to chatter. My training uniform shirt smells of dried vomit and is damp from my tears, adding to the chill. My body aches from the hunched position I've contorted into, and it whimpers in protest when I shift positions. I plead to the Fates with my last ounce of energy. *Please let someone find me.*

I hear a voice. *Is it in my head?* "Hello, is there anyone here?" I muffle through the cloth.

Silence.

So, it *was* in my head.

"Siriarna."

I hear my name whispered. "Who's there?" I say, feverishly.

"No need to fear. I am here to help you," replies the voice.

The covering is removed from my face and, even though I am still surrounded by the Void's blackness, I see a light surrounding the entity. It's Eleos, Goddess of Mercy and Compassion. I reach out to touch her to make sure I'm not hallucinating.

"How did you find me?" I stutter in disbelief.

"Siriarna, you are not like the other semi gods here on Evolirium. In time, you will see. You were put here by the three. Staying here is not meant to be. Time to rise from within. Your true journey is about to begin."

Eleos silently removes the bindings from my hands and ankles before I see her blue robes vanish.

"Wait, wait, help me, please." I yell, but I am alone again in the Void. I have no idea what the riddle she left me with means. The message is already fading from my memory.

I strain to try and remember Eleos' words and find a way out of this predicament. But all I can think about is how I got here. The way I was pulled from my bed in the middle of the night, masked and left shackled alone, causes my eyes to burn at the memory. The room suddenly seems brighter. A menacing glow emanates from the electric bolt that has somehow projected itself skyward from the bottom of the Void.

What did Eleos do?

I look down at my newly freed hands and see the purple has disappeared from my finger. Whoever did this to me has stripped my Propensity power. They have rendered me useless. It's why my chants didn't work. The syrup that was forced down my throat; that's what it did. A guttural scream escapes my lips. *No. Not my power.* I worked so hard to get into my Propensity and even harder to win the Challenge. This is more than cruel. It's evil. A new wave of tears spill, and I rock myself back and forth to try and find comfort.

******

"Siriarna?"

I hear my name. Is it in my head or is someone there, calling for me? It's hard to tell. *Am I going mad?*

"Siriarna?"

There it is again. I wait for Eleos to appear like she did before. But she does not.

"Siriarna?"

This time, I recognise Roman's voice. He's found me. "I'm down here." I cry out.

"Hang on Siriarna, I'm going to get High Power Omnisensus."

"Don't leave me." I beg. "Please don't leave me alone, Roman."

"I'll be back as fast as the speed of light. Trust me, you're safe now."

Within seconds, I recognise High Power Omnisensus' voice calling me, "Siriarna, can you hear me?"

"I'm here," I project my voice as loud as I can from the bottom of the pit.

"Hang tight, we'll have you out in no time."

Propensity Leader Xander casts a sheet of light from above, illuminating the Void. Earth Leader Lucinda wields an alchemical ladder and propels it downwards. It lands at my feet. Without hesitation, I start to climb. It's more difficult than I imagined. I am dizzy, weak, and dehydrated, so I take it slow and steady. Just when I think I can't take another step, a hand reaches mine and drags me to the top. Roman!

"Hey, stranger."

I collapse into his arms.

"Roman, take her to the medics office immediately," instructs High Power Omnisensus.

Once in the office, I try to recount the events that took place three days ago. That's what they told me—*three* days. It seemed like an eternity.

The medic pronounces me physically fine, minus a slight chill and dehydration. I am given a fluid concoction from the Alchemy Laboratory to alleviate, and counteract, the effects of both conditions. She takes note of my missing Propensity-coloured finger, runs some tests, and confirms my Propensity magic is gone. She also insists I stay in the infirmary overnight to recuperate. I don't see the point. Now my powers are gone, I have no purpose being in this realm.

"How are you feeling?"

It's Roman coming in to check on me.

"Useless."

"Don't say that. You're safe and after some rest, you'll be fine."

"How can you say that Roman? I will *not* be fine. It has

taken years to get to Propensity level and I worked so hard to make the grade. Now, it's all gone. I don't think I'll ever recover."

"I know you will. You are the smartest person I know, and you won the challenge without using any magic. You used your brain, that's your real power. Trust me," he says optimistically.

I can't meet his eyes. Optimism eludes me. Memories of the challenge cast a shadow. My vision is tunnelled to a bleak future. One without purpose, without magic and without joy. Misery binds itself to my being, hollowing out my soul. "I need to rest now," I say rolling onto my side to face the wall.

Frowning, he stands and leaves me in peace. Although, peace is the last thing I feel and wonder if I will ever find it again. There is no place on Evolirium for a semi god with no powers.

Early the next morning, I summon High Power Omnisensus. "I want to know who did this to me," I demand.

"I understand you're upset Siriarna. Please know we are investigating. I'm sorry it took so long for us to find you. There was a glamour veil covering the opening of the

Void concealing it from magic. Although strangely, it seems something powerful punched a hole through its centre. Our locator spells alerted us of your position just as Roman came to find me.

"This is a serious misconduct, and I will get to the bottom of it. The culprit will be severely punished. I will not have this kind of behaviour in my realm.

"For now, there is an administration position available in the Knowledge Room. Why don't you work there for the time being? It may help you transition ..."

"No, no, no. I can't. I won't." I yell while shaking my head uncontrollably.

My vocal outburst propels the Authority toward me. Placing a big comforting hand on my shoulder, he says, "Perhaps you should consider returning to the Home Realm. Temporarily of course. Just until you are feeling better. You are always welcome on Evolirium, and we would love to have you back when you're up to it."

The thought of returning to the Home Realm powerless threatens to send me spiralling into an even further depressive state. It especially hurts knowing I just won the end of year Propensity Challenge. The memory causes silent tears to slide from my eyes. I don't even try to wipe them away. No, I will not be returning to that realm. Though my vision is clouded by liquid, the decision is clear. I know where I need to go, there's really only one choice: The Between.

As my physical condition has stabilized, I tell High Power Omnisensus I want to leave immediately. He tries to convince me to say goodbye to my peers, but I can't. I've lost my spark and I don't want to see *anyone* before I go. I just want to slip out undetected and forget this realm altogether.

With a hollow soul and a steady hand, I unfasten the crest lapel pin, place it on the side table, and walk from the room. No looking back. Goodbye Evolirium.

******

Roman

She looked so vulnerable when she came out of the Void, just like the first day I met her in the Knowledge Room. Her eyes were the first thing I noticed, the pale violet drew me in, and I felt immediately protective. As I spent more time with her, I grew to know the kind and bright soul that defines her essence. To discover someone kidnapped her from her bed and dumped her into the Void, infuriates me.

Who would want to hurt Siriarna? I mean, she is no threat to anyone here. Her powers are growing but they are not top tier, and she wouldn't hurt a fly.

Could the challenge win have been the catalyst? If it was, why was Braxton untouched?

Whoever it was meant business because the Void is not something you mess with. What I can't grasp is how they managed to get her down there. Centuries ago, the students who played the prank on Zeus were barely functioning when he eventually returned to release them. The depth, the isolation, the lack of nourishment, and freezing cold conditions, were enough to render even a semi god serious damage. Because of this, no one has ever breached the rules and crossed over the stone wall to the Void... ever. *Not until now.*

If it wasn't for the bright light transcending from the Void, I would never have found her. It was lucky I was leaving the Learning Facility and close enough to see it, otherwise she might still be stranded there, and who knows for how long? I shudder at the thought. That brings me to another thought–w*here did that light come from?* Siriarna was alone in the Void.

When I return to visit her in the infirmary, the medic advises she has left the realm. High Power Omnisensus confirms this when I barge into his office unannounced.

Then I see her lapel pin on his desk, and I know she's gone for good. For a moment my heart stops, silently acknowledging the best friend I have lost.

CHAPTER 18

Braxton

Mount Olympus was just as palatial as I had imagined. However, I couldn't enjoy it properly without Siriarna. I tried to seek the gods' assistance in finding her and I thought I may have succeeded with Athena, but the notion was ultimately dismissed. From that point, my thoughts were consumed with leaving the realm without offending the gods—after all, my life goal is to work with them as part of The Core.

I did, however, begrudgingly enjoy the nectar. Even though I have a secret stash to trade on Evolirium, this was my first sample of the gods' drink. It is my tool to take my Propensity power to the next level, and I don't want to mess with that—regardless of how euphoric the liquid tastes.

As soon as Alexandraya returned to the table from her escapade, which seemed to take an infinite amount of time come to think of it, I requested our return to Evolirium. The look she shot me was pure venom, but I put up with the pretence long enough, and wanted out. I do not bow down to bullies.

Now back in the Progression Realm, I proceed straight to High Power Omnisensus' quarters to see if there is any update on Siriarna's whereabouts. To my absolute relief, she has been found safe. However, I was disgusted to find out she was held at the bottom of the Void. Who, in their right mind, would put another semi god there against their will? It's just too cruel to comprehend.

When I ask the Authority if I can see her, he informs me of her choice to leave Evolirium and live out her existence in The Between. He then tells me of her loss of Propensity powers. This news rocks me to my core. I am so angry and heartbroken for her. I plead with the Authority to send me to The Between, even if only for a few hours. I need to see her. I want to tell her she'll be okay, that I will always be there for her, that we can work out her future here, on Evolirium. But he refuses. He tells me her choice was to be left alone and he will respect her decision.

I am totally frustrated. I cannot accept that I will never see her again. If I could turn back time I would, but it would not change the outcome of Siriarna's magic loss. And I absolutely cannot for the life of me endure returning to the Sky Realm and spending another second with Alexandraya.

******

Alexandraya

That was the best experience of my existence. I never wanted to leave, and I wouldn't have if Braxton hadn't dragged me out the minute I returned to the table. Pining for Siriarna. That stupid girl is still bothering me, even though she is currently out of the picture.

The moment Iris landed the chariot on Mount Olympus, I felt like I was home. The opulence, the grandeur, the palace, it's everything I imagined and more. I see myself fitting into this realm and I will do anything to switch my status from semi god to god.

Anything!

I want the glory, the power and the eternal position that becoming a god will allow, and I'm positive it is within my reach. Hermes couldn't take his eyes off me this evening. Proven when he escorted me to the powder room. Which, incidentally, I never made it to. Instead, he swept me onto a private balcony and told me how much he admired me, before pulling me into an intoxicating kiss. It was more euphoric than the nectar. It took every ounce of willpower to pull away. He wants me, as I knew he would, but I have no intention of becoming one of his playthings. No, that will not suit my plan... I want to become his wife.

Before I abruptly left, he whispered in my ear that he'd like to see me again. I coolly responded that tonight was nice, but I was already taken by a semi god on Evolirium. I could see the challenge cross his eyes. A god vs semi god. No challenge at all.

Let the game begin.

The whole evening couldn't have gone any more perfectly. I hug myself in self-congratulation. I can't wait to tell Melodie and Davina how well the plan worked.

More importantly, I am looking forward to seeing Hermes again. I know it won't be too long before he makes his move.

CHAPTER 19

Siriarna

Whilst it is definitely not a nirvana like Evolirium, The Between is not as awful as I had expected. It's just a bland, and smaller by comparison, working realm. The topography is flat and city-like with intertwining tree-lined streets and low-rise buildings. Everything is grey, the foliage of the trees being the only exception. In fact, it matches my now colourless new life.

I locate my designated accommodations in the mid-realm; a tiny level 1 apartment that is just as dreary as the realm itself. Before heading up to the apartment, I stop at the food stall below and select a bottle of stream water. It's not mountain elixir—that was gift from the mountains of

Evolirium and I miss having a supply in my refrigerator. I try to drag my thoughts away from my former realm. I have no powers, no use, and no intention of returning to Evolirium.

I let out a deep sigh upon entering the tiny space. My bed is in one corner of the large room that is my new home. It's been a long day, and I climb into bed grateful that it's finally over. My slumber takes me to the night of my kidnap, and I wake screaming into the pillow. I stay awake the rest of the night too afraid my dreams will return to real life nightmares.

Finally, the sun peaks through the only window, indicating morning has arrived, relieving my fruitless attempts at sleep. I force myself to get dressed and leave the apartment. I want to explore The Between and see if there's anything I can find affinity with. After all, it was *my* choice to move here.

Leaving the building I am transfixed, mesmerised by the wet weather—it doesn't rain on Evolirium. I hold out my palms and let the gentle patter of moisture soak into my skin. The droplets tickle as they land, and I laugh out loud. The noise sounds foreign in my head, like a lost memory bubbling to the surface. *Gods let there be hope.*

The streets are mostly vacant, all mortals in the realm are busy fulfilling their purpose—working the lands, storing information, and crafting for the gods. There is no magic in The Between, so I resign myself to the fact that this is the best place for me. And I theorise it's probably best I find something to keep me busy. That should help take my mind off the powers I have lost.

Spotting a ring of benches in a sphere-shaped open court, I sit for a moment. I am alone in the space and the silence is deafening. Leaving as quickly I as entered, I hear a group of chatter. Intrigued, I stroll toward the noise.

Coming out of a jam-packed eatery, is a group of people about my age and oddly, I catch sight of someone familiar. I can't quite place her. How could I possibly recognise anyone in this realm? The girl is smallish in statue with auburn hair pulled into a tight bun. I rack my brain to try and place her. When she absently pulls out her hairband, revealing long curly hair, it suddenly strikes me... Miriam. The semi god found floating in the Zen River on Evolirium. I rush to catch the group and tap the girl lightly on her shoulder.

She spins around to face me, "Yes?"

I clear my throat, immediately lost for words. I am

standing, staring, still in shock at seeing her here in The Between. The last image I had of her was face down in the water—my body convulses in an involuntary shudder.

"Siriarna, is that you? What are you doing here?" she interrupts my awkward silence.

"Yes, it's me." I reply in a tight, high-pitched voice.

"You guys go ahead, I'll catch up with you later," Miriam says to her friends, picking up on my distress. "What are you doing here?"

I burst into tears.

Miriam immediately hugs me. "Why don't we have a little chat?"

Nodding my agreement, she leads me into the eatery she just vacated, weaving us expertly through the crowds to a small table at the back.

"Sorry about before," I say now composed. "It's just that I was shocked to see a familiar face. I wasn't expecting it."

"I'm *glad* you ran into me." She responds winking.

I laugh for the second time in as many days, and I find my soul slightly less hollow.

"When did you arrive?" She asks.

"Yesterday."

"Ah, that's why you're feeling overwhelmed. The Between is very different to Evolirium. It takes a while to adjust to the faster no-nonsense pace."

"I don't think I'll ever get used to it." I sigh.

"It's really not that bad. I mean, sure, you need to love grey..." she winks again, and I stifle another laugh. "But everything is within walking distance. Train stations are dotted throughout the mid-realm grid so it's easy to get around. Once you get used to it, you'll learn to appreciate the succinctness of the realm," she concludes.

A waitress interrupts our reunion and sets down a pitcher of bright amber liquid and two glasses. I look at Miriam. "Freshly squeezed strawberry and mango juice," she says.

My stomach growls in response. How fortunate that I ran into her today. Was it pure coincidence? I silently thank the Fates.

"Thank you, Miriam." I say, my mouth twisting into a small smile.

"I need to get back to work now but I have a great idea."

"What's that?"

"I'm going to escort you to the Festival of Gratitude

this weekend. What do you say?"

I can't accept quickly enough and nod my response.

******

Miriam arrives at my apartment the morning of the Festival of Gratitude. She looks happy and vibrant. A direct contrast to the last time I saw her on Evolirium.

"So, what is this festival all about anyway?"

"Isn't it obvious... gratitude," she laughs.

"Ah, right, 'course, it is," I say sarcastically.

"You'll see. Come on, we don't want to be late and miss the opening."

Miriam hooks her arm through mine and pulls me out the door in a mad rush. It leaves me wondering what kind of opening a gratitude festival warrants.

We walk the short distance from my apartment to the end of the city grid, where the mid-realm above ground light-rail station is located. Within minutes, the passenger train has arrived, and we commence our journey to the outskirts. The farming lands are dedicated to fulfilling food supplies to the gods and I'm excited to see something other than the grey of mid-realm.

During the trip, I work up the courage to speak to Miriam about past events. "I know this might be prying, and I'm sorry if I am, but I would really like to know what happened to you on Evolirium."

Miriam takes a deep breath and exhales before starting her story... "I was happy and popular on Evolirium, and I was on track to top all my classes before Propensity Selection. The lecturers favoured me, and everyone knew I was set to lead future assignments, both reconnaissance and missions. I was leaning toward Time or Earth Propensities—both genuinely interested me for different reasons. Choosing a Propensity seemed to be my biggest issue. Well, so I thought."

She stops her story momentarily, as the train click clacks over the elemental power station.

"Please go on, Miriam," I say as the journey resumes its smooth passage.

"During an advanced workshop for gifted students, I was selected to conjure a chain and bind a fellow student. It was a high-level chant. I could hear sneering behind me, but I brushed it off because I knew I could do it. I stepped up to the front of the class alongside the designated student and began. The chains appeared, weaving around the student's wrists and ankles as instructed. But instead of stopping there, they continued to rattle and clank, entwining the student head to toe. The chaos created a class uproar with outbursts of hysterical laughter. The lecturer had to step in to stop the chant and release the chains, because the student was having trouble breathing. She was so angry. She pledged to have her revenge and silenced the class with her verbal animosity. You should have heard the venom in her voice. It was frightening."

The train stops at the farming lands station. People are clamouring to disembark, interrupting Miriam's narration. I am, literally, sitting on the edge of my seat straining to hear her story over the noise. The suspense is killing me.

"Come on Siriarna, let's go."

Miriam jumps up, following the crowd. I have no choice but to follow her. Her excitement is contagious, so I push her story to the back of my mind and concentrate on the events that are about to unfold.

A wave of people gathers around the outside of a vast empty field. Miriam expertly manoeuvres us into a superior vantage position. "We made it, it's about to begin," she says, squeezing my hand.

I see nothing but an empty field. I try to pretend I am just as eager as she is, and force a smile. Within seconds, a loud bang echoes, smoke shrouds the fields, and the crowd erupts in voracious cheers.

I have no idea what's going on... then I see it. A large chariot emerges from the haze. I've never seen anything like it. It stands tall and proud in all its glory; the craftsmanship is superb. A bright flash of light signals the arrival of God Apollo, who is now standing at the helm of his new golden chariot. He throws a ball of light into the sky above, takes out his bow and arrow and shoots a spear through its centre. The ball explodes into thousands of tiny snowflakes. My mouth drops in awe.

"I told you it was something else," Miriam grins.

She explains the annual festival celebrates the labour of workers in The Between and is centred around a different god each year, this year being Apollo. His gift, the glorious new chariot, took artisans the entire year to proudly complete.

Apollo takes his time to speak to festival goers, particularly paying attention to the children of the realm, who lap up the sheer magnificence of his presence. It really is a spectacle not to be missed, and I'm glad Miriam invited me.

After the snowflakes dissipate, food tables are wheeled into the centre of the fields. Freshly farmed fruits and vegetables are on display, together with exotic looking refreshments. I help myself to a mouth-watering scented vegetable dish wrapped in a banana leaf, and a sky-blue coloured fruit cocktail. Miriam grabs the same. We find a space along a fence to lean against while we consume the appetising cuisine.

"Thank you for bringing me here, Miriam. I'm actually having a great time. And this truly is the most delicious food I have ever tasted." I say with gratitude.

"You're welcome. The food is the best thing about this realm. So fresh. Only the best for our gods." She winks.

Music from the band playing in the north field, is carried through the atmosphere by the light breeze. A flock of people dance freely in front of us, not a care in the realm, and children's laughter echoes throughout the space. The festival is in full swing now, and I'm enchanted by the celebrations. It's exactly what I needed to inject some life back into my damaged soul.

Out of the blue, I hear my name spoken.

"Interesting. I didn't think I would be seeing you here,

Siriarna."

I whirl around to find Apollo towering over me. How does he know who I am? We have never met. "I can't say I thought I'd be here either," I respond matter-of-factly.

He laughs—a great audacious guffaw. It fits his sheer size and magnificence. "You are quite the enigma. I must say, I did find it intriguing when the boy asked Athena for her assistance in finding you. It was a bold move to ask a favour of a god, and Athena is particularly pedantic. Of course, she declined his request. But you don't seem to be misplaced any longer, I see."

I have no idea what he's talking about.

What boy and how did he know I was missing?

I'm about to ask Apollo this very question when I remember the Evolirium Challenge reward dinner. Braxton must have attended without me. My heart flip flops in my chest as I remember the last time I saw him and *that* kiss.

"The dinner," I reply, temporarily distracted.

"Yes. Hermes was quite taken with your replacement, so all was not lost."

My what? Someone went in my place.

Before the words are even out of my mouth, I know

exactly who it was—Alexandraya.

Apollo seems bored now. He has turned his back and is walking away toward his gleaming new chariot. Before he gets too far away, I ask him the question that had me curious the moment he addressed me.

"Your Greatness, can I please ask how you know who I am?"

His response floors me. "Eleos—she seems to think you have a higher purpose."

I can't ask anything further because he has vanished. I have a million thoughts swimming through my mind. I don't know where to start, or how to sort them into any kind of sense. I clutch my temples that are now aching with confusion. Miriam grabs my hand and pulls me to a vacant space.

"What was that all about Siriarna? Do you know Apollo?"

"No, I've never met him or any god. Oh, wait, I have. Sort of. Kind of." I reply flustered, thinking back to Eleos who came to me at the bottom of the Void, relaying that strange message. Then there was Hermes, after my one and only mission.

"Take a deep breath. You don't look so good," she

instructs after scanning my pallid skin tone.

All heat has evaporated from my body, and I'm starting to shiver despite the pleasant realm temperature. "You know, I think I'm going to leave."

"I'll come with you," Miriam insists.

With a tight smile, I tell her to stay and enjoy the festivities. She tries to argue with me. But I silence her with a stiff hug, before stomping from the field. Visions of the Void haunting my thoughts.

******

Back in my apartment, I try to piece together what took place at the festival. A knock at the door interrupts that task. It's Miriam.

"Hey, I thought you were staying at the festival," I say ushering her inside and over to my tiny couch, where we cram in together tightly.

"No chance. I wasn't about to leave you alone after what happened. That was truly bizarre, and more than a little intriguing. I think it's time to spill."

"Where do I start?" I sigh.

"How about with how and why you came to The

Between? Oh, and Eleos... and what did you mean about the dinner?" She is speaking so quickly her words are rambling together.

"Okay, here goes everything . . ."

I start by telling Miriam about the Challenge win. Then I explain part of the prize was a dinner with the gods on Mount Olympus.

"So that's why Apollo mentioned your replacement."

"Yes, I think so. My best guess is that it was Alexandraya."

Miriam gasps, "Of course it was," she says sarcastically.

My mouth has become dry. I swallow the lump forming in my throat before proceeding with the events that brought about my inhabitancy in this realm. Through a high-pitched voice that sounds foreign in my head, I continue speaking, starting with the kidnapping— how I was wrenched from my bed in the obscured nocturnal hours. My voice drops to a whisper when I mention the Void.

I feel a light squeeze in my palm and look down to see that Miriam has picked up my right hand with both of hers. The gesture helps me persevere.

I resume the narrative with the appearance of Eleos

and the cryptic message she conveyed before vanishing. Finally, I tell her about my rescue, and the loss of my Propensity power. That being the catalyst for my decision to relocate to The Between.

At some point during the story, I abstractedly pulled my legs to my chest and wrapped my arms around them. Just like I did in the Void.

Miriam's normally sunny disposition has turned thunderous. She reaches over and dabs the tears I didn't realise had trickled from my eyes with the back of her sleeve. "I'm sorry that happened to you, too."

My stomach twists into a knot. "Too?"

"I was also taken from my hut in the middle of the night. Then dumped in the Zen River," she says tightly.

"Oh Miriam, I remember that awful day. It was one of the worst things to have ever happened on an otherwise peaceful Evolirium. Did you see who did that to you? Do you know who it was?" I ask desperately.

"No, I didn't see anything. It all happened so quickly. Before I knew it, High Power Omnisensus was fishing me out of the water. Even though I hadn't then chosen my Propensity and received my coloured finger, my magic was eradicated. Whoever was responsible took everything from me. The whole stupid stunt nearly cost me my life. What's ironic is that I wish I could return to Evolirium. I still feel like a part of me is missing. The memory of my former magic still haunts me."

Miriam's anguish mirrors my own. I miss my power. Even though average and unpredictable, I feel naked without it. Lost. And I also miss Evolirium. Try as I might to forget it, my thoughts habitually wander there—to Roman, and Braxton... especially Braxton.

Reining in those faraway thoughts, a random question pops into my mind, "Who was the girl you bound in chains on Evolirium?"

"Alexandraya," she responds, and we both look at each other in a lightbulb moment.

"Do you think the TON were responsible? There were so many rumours saying they were guilty straight after your incident."

"The TON?" Miriam says tilting her head to the side, brows drawing together.

"It stands for 'Trio of Nightmares'. It's the name I made up for Alexandraya, Melodie and Davina when I first arrived on Evolirium," I say embarrassed.

Miriam stifles a giggle, despite the misery of reliving her

past trauma. "I thought so at first because Alexandraya openly threatened me in the classroom and both Melodie and Davina do everything she demands. I begged High Power Omnisensus to investigate my theory. He soon confirmed Alexandraya was spotted with both Melodie and Davina at the Etherial Room at the time of my incident, therefore ruling her out of any involvement. I left the realm the following day."

I digest Miriam's response. Something doesn't quite sit right. It's way too convenient an alibi. I'd go so far as to say it was premeditated. "I'm sorry that happened to you Miriam."

"It's okay Siriarna. I've made a good life here in The Between. You'll see. You will, too."

The exhaustion of the day's events starts to take a toll, and my eyelids fight to stay open. Miriam stands to leave but before she does, makes one final observation. "Siriarna, gods do not make the time to mix with semi gods. Even if one is missing. Eleos coming to you in the Void is odd. And then there's the fact that she has spoken to Apollo about you. Why do you think that is?"

"I have no clue," I respond honestly. However, this is something I plan on finding out. And sooner, rather than later. Then I will get to the bottom of finding out who it was that took everything from me.

CHAPTER 20

Siriarna

It's been a month now since I banished myself to The Between. The pace of the realm is fast, business-like, and purposeful. Miriam found me a position working with her in the Pharmakeia which has kept me busy and given me a new sense of worth.

"Morning," she says brightly.

"That it is." I laugh.

It's our daily ritual.

I pull out my lab coat from the worker's room cupboard. It's grey like everything else in the realm, but I am akin to Miriam wearing it, and her positive essence lifts my spirit.

Today we are preparing a growth enhancement feed additive for the livestock in the realm. Mixing the ingredients in a mortar and pestle is the closest thing to Earth Propensity. Whilst nostalgic, the task also brings with it a sense of sorrow.

"I love mixing these ingredients. If I close my eyes, I imagine I'm back in the Alchemical Laboratory." Miriam says while humming.

I'm grinding my ingredients with such force, completely lost in the past, when the Pharmakeia experiences a blackout. A mutual groan from the production line reverberates around the laboratory as work grinds to a halt. My eyes begin to burn, and the room brightens. Blackout over.

A collective cheer sounds from the workers.

Miriam turns to me and says, "That was strange." Then noticing my expression, "Siriarna, are you okay?"

"I don't know."

I was so engrossed in grinding the compound when the room unexpectedly went black. I simply thought about the lights, wishing they would illuminate, and they did.

Was I responsible? Have my powers returned?

"You don't look so good." She moves quickly behind

me, in time to catch me as I faint. "I think we'd better get you home," she says as I regain consciousness.

In my apartment, Miriam brings me a glass of water, "Wanna tell me what happened back in the lab?"

"I think my magic is returning, or at least some form of power." I say in a whisper, afraid of speaking my theory out loud.

"W-what? How can that be?"

I share with her all the strange incidents that have happened to me over this past year, before I came to The Between; from flickering lights to shattering bulbs, ending with the blackout in the lab this morning.

"Unbelievable, but amazing Siriarna," she says wide-eyed. "Do you have any idea why you were able to access this power in the first place, and why it's happening again now?"

"No. I wish I did."

A memory from my Surface World mission rematerializes. Ms M clairvoyant predicted my psychokinesis would emerge once my mind was clear. I share this information with Miriam.

"Do you think this power was what Eleos and Apollo were referring to?" Miriam questions.

"I have absolutely no idea. What I do know is that I have no control over when it happens, nor the manner of force behind it when it occurs."

"I would want to know if my magic was returning." Miriam says wistfully.

I shoot her a sympathetic smile, "I think I'm ready to find out. Will you help me?

"Of course! I think we should start with your lineage. It might give us a starting point as to why you are having these 'mind surges'," she suggests.

"It's a good thought, but only Goddess Eileithyia holds such information. And she is forbidden to disclose it to anyone, including the Gods, by order of the Fates."

"True, but she must keep that information somewhere. And Siriarna, we're going to find it."

The look of determination on her face fills me with hope. She has, without a doubt, been the best thing about living in The Between—reconnecting with her has been an unexpected godsend. While I am no longer the same trusting person of the past, I credit Miriam's friendship in helping me heal. However, I still cling to the hope that I will one day have my revenge on whoever was responsible for leaving me damaged. The possibility of my magic returning is a surprise and if triumphant, will help me achieve the justice I crave. "I guess I'll be heading to the archives tomorrow, then. Will you cover me at the Pharmakeia?"

"Like you have to ask," her mouth turns upwards into a widespread grin. "This is the most exciting thing I've been involved in since I arrived in this realm—a birthright quest. I'm thrilled for you Siriarna."

I have never wanted to know which god was my 'real' parent. My guide parents are amazing and that has always been enough. I love going to the Home Realm at the end of each training year and spending my break reconnecting with them. I know the other students on Evolirium used to talk and gossip about which god they belonged to, but that discussion never interested me. Even when Linus and Stefanie annoyed me, I still never once thought about my true heritage.

The only time I ever gave thought to godly lineage, was when I heard rumours Zeus was Roman's father. I don't know how those rumours started, but as the weeks passed by, Roman seemed to be transcending into more than a semi god. Thus, proving some validity to the claims. Deep down, this bothered me. If it were found to be true and he was the son of Zeus and another god or minor deity, Roman could choose to leave Evolirium and inhibit Mount Olympus, as an heir entitled god.

Back then, when I started to worry about this possibility, I didn't know I was the one set to leave Evolirium for good—decided by another, in a horribly vengeful act.

******

I laid awake all night consumed with the hope that my powers might be returning. I concentrated all my efforts on trying to produce a flicker in the apartment lights to no avail. I tried blinking, opening my eyes wide, squinting. Everything. It didn't work. Not even a hint of magic surfaced. Surrendering, I stared blankly at the ceiling, willing myself to sleep—a pointless effort.

Even though tired, I'm running on pure adrenalin this morning. I am desperate to get to the archives and start the search into my elusive heritage. Replacing my normal realm grey attire, I dress in my black mission uniform to harness the right mindset. Now thankful I threw it in with the limited belongs I packed when I relocated to The

Between. Subconsciously I must have known I would need it. A personal mission, I smile at the irony.

The archive building is just around the corner from my apartment, and I slip in unseen. The old building is one of the original structures of mid-realm and not popular with residents. I bypass the electronic archives and navigate my way through the labyrinth of stacks. What I'm looking for is original scrolls or manuscripts that may house the location of Eileithyia.

Breathing in the dusty air triggers a sneeze to escape my nose and mouth.

"Gods' bless you."

I turn to find a peppy employee lurking behind me. "Thank you."

"Can I help you find something?"

I think twice about whether I should ask this young boy for his help in finding what I need. "I'm trying to find the location of a god." I say deciding it couldn't hurt.

"Cool. Which one?"

"Eileithyia."

"You'd need to start over here, in offspring of Olympian Gods." He rambles on about the gods and their various power, and how awesome he thinks they are, for the longest time. It's obvious he doesn't get many visitors in the archives. "So, I guess I'll leave you to it," he says finally, spent of breath.

I give him a grateful smile and, finally, start my search.

Just before nightfall, I find what I'm looking for. An old manuscript depicting only a symbol of a woman wielding a torch, embossed on the outside. I know this is the mark representing Eileithyia. With shaking hands, I open the manuscript. The pages are filled with symbols only. And I know how to decipher them! Stefanie was right—for the first time in my life, I am truly grateful for my photographic memory.

It takes longer than I had imagined, but I eventually come across the answers I seek. "Yes." I speak out loud to the empty aisle.

The employee, who was hovering in nearby stacks, wanders over to my position when he hears my elated utterance. "Find what you needed?" he asks intrigued.

"Yes, I absolutely did." I say grinning. Although, my smile instantly turns upside down.

"You don't look too happy," he says shrewdly.

Now I have an idea of Eileithyia's whereabouts, I've no idea how to summon a chariot to get from The Between to the Surface Realm. "I don't suppose you know how I might contact a chariot," I say flippantly.

"Actually, I do."

In all honesty, this is not the answer I had expected. "Do you think you might be able to help me?"

"You know what... I think I can."

******

Humming, I walk through the busy thoroughfares to the eatery where I'm meeting Miriam. The same eatery she exited from the day I found her in this realm. It has become my favourite retreat in The Between.

She is already seated when I arrive. "Did you find anything of interest?" she asks, her eyes glittering with anticipation.

"I did." I break into a huge smile.

"For gods' sake Siriarna, don't keep me waiting," she laughs.

I tell her that I didn't find any information on semi god birth parents, but I was able to ascertain Eileithyia is in Knossos on the Surface World.

"That's an amazing start to your quest Siriarna."

My quest.

My stomach twists in knots at the thought of embarking on a journey no semi god has ever succeeded in before me. I am pioneering my heritage.

"How are you going to travel through realms?"

"Well, here's the thing... turns out Cyrus' uncle is the Realm Master.

"Cyrus?"

"He was the Archivian that helped me find Eileithyia's manuscript. He's quite devoted to the gods and the Sky Realm."

"I mean, what are the chances of that?"

"I know. I can't quite believe my luck."

"Things are falling into place, Siriarna. Just like they're meant to. I truly believe that. It's almost like the Fates are watching or something."

A shiver runs down my spine when Miriam mentions the Fates. I brush it off as a weird coincidence.

"Miriam, I don't know what I would have done without you here. I'm going to miss you. Very much." I bite my tongue to stop myself from bursting into thankful tears.

"I'm going to miss you too Siriarna. Please be careful

and come back safely." She squeezes me tightly, "I hope you really do have your magic back."

"Me too," I whisper

I make a silent promise to myself that if I do have access to my magic, I will do everything within my power to help return hers.

******

Early the next morning, I board the chariot to the Surface World. *My future awaits. Or is it my past?*

CHAPTER 21

Siriarna

It feels strange entering the Surface World at Knossos. Particularly as I have arrived before dawn to a still sleeping, and quietened realm. Last time I had the backup of my mission group, but this time I am alone, seeking answers from an elusive god. And this makes me nervous. Especially as so many semi gods have failed in their search for answers before me.

The manuscript I found in the archives sited Eileithyia's location to be her place of birth; The Cave of Amnisos. That's where I am headed now.

According to the symbols I deciphered, the cave entrance is located down a winding pathway next to a giant fig tree. The tree bestows a creative energy to those who touch it and when in fruit, the fig signals fertility. It's a magical gift from the Goddess Eileithyia.

Following the path, I locate the place where the entrance should be, but find myself facing a solid rock face. Circling the slab, I find no way to enter. In fact, it is not a cave at all. Puzzled, I sit on one of the surrounding boulders perplexed. From my lowered position, the first morning sun's rays shine onto the rock highlighting an indent in the otherwise smooth exterior. Rising and moving to the anomaly, I trail my hands over the imperfection and encounter a spike. I've read about these spikes being ancient rites of passage requiring a blood sacrifice. I never, in my wildest dreams, expected to find one in existence.

Here goes nothing.

Holding my breath, I press my index finger onto the spike until it draws a droplet of blood. A small hidden doorway materialises, and I squeeze through the gap without a backward glance. Once inside, the doorway vanishes behind me. I'm trapped inside this place. Gods, I hope Eileithyia is here.

The darkened space sends me into a blind panic,

bringing back memories of the Void, and my throat constricts. I start to hum softly. The vibrations calm my body and I force myself to push onwards and focus on my mission.

Moving forward, I raise my eyes upward and sight clusters of tiny stalactites hanging from the cave ceiling, glowing like little mineral candles. As my eyes readjust to the dim light, I hesitantly walk down the rocky staircase in front until my feet find flattened earth and a long narrow hallway. I try to ignore the beat of my pounding heart in the silence, but the rapid thumping is hard to abandon. Leaning up against the cave wall, I slide forward cautiously taking small, steady steps under the natural hanging candle lights. It's not long before an opening appears, brightened by a hollowed out rock cavity reaching the skies above. The sight gives my body a minor reprieve.

In the centre of the lightened space lies the worship stone with two stalagmites erupting from the earth beside it—the stones signifying mother and child. I reach out a hand to touch the minerals. The texture is oddly smooth and the symbolism causes me to tremble. Ultimately, I am here to find the identity of my birth god and the magnitude of this purpose is suddenly overwhelming.

A voice echoes around the chamber and I snatch my hand away from the stalagmite.

"I wondered the day you would seek me, Siriarna."

Eileithyia emerges and lights a central torch, further illuminating the chamber around us.

I recoil at the arrival of the goddess.

"No need to be scared," she says.

With a shaky voice, I ask, "How do you know who I am?"

"I knew one day you would come. And in light of recent events, I knew it would be soon."

"So you know why I am here?"

"I do."

"I need some answers. Will you tell me who my god parent is?"

"The Fates have sworn me to secrecy regarding semi god births, but your case is one for the rules to break. Follow me into my living chambers, there is much to discuss."

The gravity of Eileithyia willing to reveal this sacred information causes my heart to quiver. I am about to discover the truth, the answer to a forbidden question. I stumble in my haste. *Could I be more awkward?*

The goddess' chamber is nothing like the central alter. It is a contrast of luxury. The dirt floor has been replaced with intricate marble, and multiple tapestries hang from the walls. There are rich jewelled coloured velvet chairs with woven rugs beneath them covering the floor. It's an underground palace, and I'm speechless.

Eileithyia beckons me to a chair. "What I am about to divulge will be of some shock to you. It will give you the answers you seek but will leave you a different person to who you believe you are now."

"I'm ready," I say humbly.

"I will start at the beginning... Many centuries ago, here on Knossos, a beautiful mortal princess started capturing the attention of the population and their worship soon followed. As the hoard grew, word made way to Goddess Aphrodite who was extremely displeased. She instructed her faithful son to compel the princess into falling in love with an average mortal, then hide herself away from society.

"Instead, Eros fell in love with the princess and could not bear to see her married to another. He wanted her for himself. He took his proposal of marriage to Zeus. Then he pleaded for immortality for his bride, so he could be bound to her for all eternity. Zeus agreed with the unusual request–it was the only time in history a god had requested the hand of a mortal, and he was intrigued.

"Unbeknown to Eros, Zeus planned to see first-hand the power this princess held over him. When he entered the Surface World and approached the princess, he too was captured by her beauty. So much so that he took her to his bed. Even though in love with Eros, the princess could not resist the Almighty Ruler. Zeus returned to Mount Olympus and forgot about the princess. He did not know he had left his seed behind.

"The princess sought my help. She was with child but wanted so desperately to marry Eros; she begged me to keep her pregnancy a secret, and take the child after its birth. She was so fragile and hysterical, I agreed with her request.

"After the wedding ceremony, the princess was offered a taste of ambrosia—food of the gods. Once ingested, her transition from mortal to god began. Days later, she feigned illness and returned to me here at Amnisos. I delivered her baby early, well before its due date and, with the help of The Fates, we froze it in time for centuries.

Until Time itself could hold it no longer. When the newborn awoke, perfect in every way despite its early delivery, I placed it in the care of guide parents. The princess never saw her baby and was unaware of the awakening 18 years ago.

"That baby was you Siriarna. You were conceived from a mortal mother who transformed into a god during your gestation. You have inherited your power from your parents—the electricity of your father combined with the power and royalty of your mother. You are quite the enigma. Your god parents are Zeus and Psyche."

I can *not* believe what has just transpired. My parents are both gods. I am not a semi god. I am a god.

I am a god!

I repeat this revelation to myself over and over, hoping it might make sense the more I hear it. *And my father is the Ruler of all Gods.*

"Now to a momentous warning. Zeus does not know of your existence—his reaction will be unpredictable. Psyche knows only that she abandoned a child from a shameful secret she has long hidden. She will not take the news of your renaissance well. Eros will not be pleased to learn of Zeus' betrayal with the love of his life."

Eileithyia places a hand on my now slumped shoulders. I don't know how to react, it's just too much. Not long ago, I was relegated to The Between after having my Propensity powers stripped. Then, out of the blue, they returned at unpredictable and inappropriate times, triggered through thought instead of chanting. Now, I find out it is because I am a god–born from the Ruler of all Gods, who doesn't know I exist. And my mother was a mortal who transformed into a god, so shamed by her wicked secret, she didn't want me. In fact, she unloved me when she delivered me early to avoid getting caught.

My eyes squeeze shut in resignation. I want to scream with frustration at the sheer magnitude of my new situation. Where am I supposed to go? Where do I fit in? What am I supposed to do now? Before I have a chance to ask Eileithyia all these questions, the burning sensation behind my eyes returns, and the pressure is building.

Oh no, not now.

There are no modern day light globes in the cave palace, only centuries old torches. I focus my attention there and a strange phenomenon happens when I release the electricity, and it hits the torch. Sparks emerge from the flame, now electrified, and they are furiously seeking an outlet to strike. I glance at a tapestry on the wall and the newly charged flame shoots toward it, setting it on fire in a burning rage. I fall to the ground, exhausted. Eileithyia quickly extinguishes the flame and comes to my aid, wrapping her robes around me.

I look up at her from the ground, tears filling my eyes.

"It's okay Siriarna. You have a great power, currently in its infancy. You need to learn how to use it effectively. I will help you. You will stay here with me until you are in control," she says soothingly.

"Why would you do this for me?"

"I have been watching over you since the day you were born. I placed you with Linus and Stefanie because I knew what a wonderful home they would provide you. I sent Eleos to you when you were in the Void. I have protected you for centuries, and I will always be here to help you."

Eileithyia guides me from the scorched living chamber to a room she says will be mine for the duration of my stay.

Before I fall asleep from both mental and physical exhaustion, I see a small portrait of an infant hanging in the corner of the room. The baby is clutching a seistron. On closer inspection, I see an initial carved into the handle, an "S". *I used to love that rattle.*

CHAPTER 22

Siriarna

Early the next morning, I wake to the smell of breakfast.

"You look like you need a good feed. When was the last time you ate?" Eileithyia chastises.

I have to think hard about this question, because I truly can't really remember. I have been running on adrenaline for so long. Even though semi gods don't consume food as often as mortals, they still need a consistent food source for optimum strength. My response is a shrug. *Do gods need the same nourishment?*

Sitting at the marble kitchen bench, I pick up a slice of breakfast pie from the feast laid out in front of me. I hadn't realised how hungry I was because I devour it in two bites. And my stomach growls in gratitude. *Mental note, gods do need to eat!*

Eileithyia nods her approval and hands me a plate of fresh fruit. "We will commence training as soon as you have finished eating."

My body stiffens at the prospect of training. I have not been able to summon my powers at will before. Plus, it has been months since I have willingly used any type of magic.

Eileithyia is waiting for me in the living chamber where there is no evidence of yesterday's disaster. She begins speaking as soon as I enter the room. "As a god, you are born with power. When you have total control, you will feel gentle vibrations course through your body—like a constant hum."

"Eileithyia, if I am a god, why has it taken so long for my powers to surface?"

She takes a deep breath and answers patiently. "Due to your mother's transition after your conception, it was not clear how your gene heritage would distribute. Under normal circumstances, there is a 50/50 split between parents. I knew for certain your genetic makeup was fifty percent god after Zeus, but the remaining fifty percent from your mother was questionable due to her mortal, then godly status.

"As time passed with no occurrence of any higher power than your Propensity, I assumed you had inherited Psyche's mortal genes, crowning you a semi god. However, I believe your eighteenth birthday was the significant turning point. Now, follow me, it's time to begin your lessons—you need to unlock your true power."

Eileithyia casts a spell and blankets us in a veil of glamour, hiding our journey along the streets from the mortals of the Surface Realm. She explains we are headed to the Archaeological Museum of Heraklion. It is a treasure of information, showcasing great statues and historical artefacts. There are many galleries, one of which is hidden, and dedicated to the gods when visiting this realm. This is our destination today.

The room houses a large oval table surrounded by chairs, with one corner allocated to a less formal lounging area. Painted frescos cover the walls depicting all gods. The centrepiece showcases Zeus upon a throne with an eagle perched on his shoulder, mortal men and women bowed in worship. I trace my fingers over the artwork and stop at my father. I stare at his features to see if I can find a resemblance. His steel grey eyes draw me in. They give the impression of a barely contained storm, and I find myself mesmerised by them.

Eileithyia places a hand on my shoulder, "It is time to release your power."

I try to do as instructed. It's hit and miss. On occasion, I am able to create a small spark and produce a small flicker in the room's light bulbs, however, it is fleeting. "I can't do this, it's useless," I say gritting my teeth.

"Of course, you can. Do not fight against it, you must embrace the power. It is your birthright," she responds.

Is it? I feel the same as I always have. Or do I? I've no idea any more.

I take a deep breath and try once again to summon my power. Nothing happens. Not even the spark I was able to produce moments ago, is duplicated. I want to scream. I want to cry. I want to run. So that's what I do. I bolt out of the museum and dart onto the stone pathway, weaving in and out of passing mortals. I pick up speed and keep moving forward, no idea where I'm headed. The air is thick and hot, and sweat forms across my brow. I slow pace and try to gather my bearings. The run has provided a much-needed clarity, wiping the mental fog from my brain.

By some miracle, I find my way back to Eileithyia's home. She is waiting for me in the living room, a jug of water and glass positioned on the table in front of her.

"I'm sorry Eileithyia. I don't know what came over me. It was just too much."

"Drink child. Tomorrow is a new day."

"I will try to do better tomorrow," I promise.

"I know you will." A small smile curves her lips.

******

Daylight brings a fresh attitude and clear mindset. I am ready to tackle today's training. Again, we make our way to the museum and into the allocated god's chamber. I come face to face with my father's portrait, but my focus has returned, and I move without loitering to the open space at the back of the room.

I start with the breathing exercises I learned on Evolirium. Next, I clear my mind and zero in on the task of creating electricity. It works and I am successfully able to manipulate the room's lighting at will. Relieved elation washes over me. *I do have my powers back and I am kind of, sort of, in control–a dream come true.*

Eileithyia calmly asks me to progress my powers by summoning electricity to my palm. I attempt the request but am unable to fulfil it. The earlier elation vanishes. The goddess notices the change in my body language, and announces we are done for the day. Without argument, I allow her to escort me back to my temporary home.

"You did well today Siriarna."

"I did okay."

"Don't be so hard on yourself. You have taken the first step, and your power is proving consistent. That is a substantial step forward."

We are sitting, well I'm slouched horizontally, on the velvet living room couches. Eileithyia narrates tales of her past semi god baby deliveries, which are fascinating. I am drawn into each story enthralled, her voice a soft, steady melody. My mind drifts to my own birth and, sensing the time is right, I ask, "Tell me about my birth."

Eileithyia obliges. "Your delivery was early and when you entered this world, you were tiny and fragile. You had a faint halo of light surrounding your being, and I knew you had a higher purpose. Your breathing stopped and I called to the Fates to spare you. They were not pleased with the summoning, but once they saw your aura, they agreed. When your breathing was strong enough, the Fates placed you in a Time capsule."

A single tear slides down my cheek. I am alive because of this goddess.

"And my mother?" I murmur.

"She knew only of your arrival, nothing more."

A twisted glimmer of hope sprouts before I fall into a deep slumber.

******

I wake famished from the constant training, and head straight to the kitchen. Eileithyia is there waiting, fruit platter laid out. She reminds me of Stefanie, and a sharp pang grips my chest. I know I can always count on my guide parents' unconditional support, but this journey of my heritage discovery, is one I must embark upon on my own.

Today, Eileithyia has decided to take my training directly outside the cave palace. In the open space, there are no light bulbs for me to manipulate. I take position in a clearing next to a cluster of trees. With calm determination, I try to focus on creating an electrical spark in my palm. I do this for more than an hour without success.

Instead of allowing my emotions to wander into a negative space, I take a break and join Eileithyia, who's sitting beneath the corridor of trees. I need time to regroup before my next attempt. She hands me an apple as I sit—more food! Crunching into the fruit, I allow my mind to relax, to breathe. A foreign sensation washes through my conscious. The mental shelves I use to store knowledge seem to be reorganising themselves—I can *feel* them. Like a chain reaction, a fresh new space has materialised. The vibration and hum that Eileithyia described is pulsing through my veins.

Without taking another bite, I drop the apple and sprint to the clearing. I am excited to try and tap into this power. It's calling to me from my internal thoughts. Standing in the open field, I concentrate on the gentle hum and energy pulsing through my veins. I locate all my power, filed neatly in its new space. The fire behind my eyes returns, but this time, I concentrate on the electricity and direct it to my palm. Static appears in the shape of a small orb. I control it, move it between each hand, and then extinguish it as quickly as it came. The headaches I have been getting instantly disappear now my power has settled into its new crevice.

I look at Eileithyia in the distance and holler as loud as I can, "I am Siriarna, and I am a god."

She rushes over and embraces me within her robes, "Yes, Siriarna, you are," she whispers.

******

Returning to the palace cave, Eileithyia and I sit for some time in silence, and I know this is the last time I will inhabit Amnisos. "You have done well Siriarna, as I knew you would," she says matter-of-factly, breaking the quiet. "Now you have control of your power, it is time for you to leave and fulfil your destiny."

I try to protest, saying I'm not ready. That I still need her guidance, but her eyes are no longer smiling back at me. Instead, they are resolved, steely, her stance firm.

Sadness grips my heart, knowing I am about to leave this woman, Goddess of Childbirth, who has been watching over me since my entry into this world—protecting my identity. She is the silent guardian I did not know I had.

I ask the last question I have for the Great Goddess, "Where do I fit in, now?"

"You are in a unique position, Siriarna. Due to your heritage, you have access to all realms. You may inhibit Mount Olympus whenever you choose without invite. The same applies to Evolirium. Lastly, due to the traits acquired from your mother's initial mortality, specifically your appearance, you can fit within the Surface World—you are by rights, a Princess of Knossos. The choice is yours from here on in. But please beware, I have kept Psyche's indiscretion a secret for centuries. Your progression to a god will unleash ramifications no one will see coming. Take care my Siriarna, you are always welcome here."

Before I leave Eileithyia hands me a magnificent amethyst pendant. The large prism-shaped stone is delicately surrounded in gold, giving it a halo-like appearance. The brilliant purple coloured stone matches my eyes; it looks like it has been custom made just for me.

"This was your mother's before she transitioned to a god. It is rightfully yours now Siriarna—I believe it was always meant for you." She kisses the top of my head and whispers, "Now go."

CHAPTER 23

Siriarna

Climbing the rungs of the suspended ladder, I board the waiting chariot, contemplating my destination. Once aboard, I stroke my amethyst pendant, and instantly know where I must travel. The charioteer shakes the reins, and the immortal horses knowingly respond to their master's command. As soon as we are airborne, the veil hiding our existence from the Surface World lifts. The wind catches my hair, blowing previously straightened bangs into my face. Automatically, I tuck them firmly behind my ears, securing them into place.

Within moments we are exiting the vortex, and the heavenly welcome of Mount Olympus immediately comes into view. Oversized golden gates open automatically, and I crane my neck to watch them close behind.

No turning back now!

The horses hit the ground with nothing more than a whisper of hooves. Past the Main Palace they gallop—the House of Zeus. My father's residence. Trepidation strikes as we gallop past. I know I will face him soon, however, today's journey is dedicated to my reunion with Psyche. *Gods help me.*

The chariot comes to a standstill outside a lavish and rather ostentatious palace. Solid gold inlays snake through the building's elaborate mouldings, and angelic carvings sit audaciously on prominent corbels. Eros and Psyche's home. I suck a sharp breath into my lungs as the brashness of my actions register. Heart pounding, I jump from the chariot, head held high, and walk to my mother's front door.

Wrapping my knuckles on the large ancient oak door, I make barely a sound. Instead of continuing the charade redundantly, I slide the wooden bolt from its housing and let myself into the palace entrance hall, completely unannounced.

"Hello" I call out.

Nothing. No response is met by my greeting. I try again. This time, I take a deep breath and project my voice as loud as I can.

"Hel-lo."

I hear footsteps approach from afar. In almost an instant, standing right in front of me, is Psyche herself. She is every bit as beautiful as her legend portrays. Pale flawless skin, full rosy lips, and the bluest sapphire eyes sparking within her angelic face. The most astonishing feature is the faint glittering outline of butterfly wings sprouting from her back. I am in awe at her magnificence and have trouble grasping that this goddess is really my mother.

Her voice brings me back to reality.

"Can I help you?" she asks in a sweet melodic pitch.

Here it is—the moment I hadn't realised I have been waiting for my entire life. "My name is Siriarna, and I was hoping we could speak."

"What a strange request, Siriarna. It is not common practice for a semi god to appear at the palace of a god. In fact, it is forbidden without invitation."

"That is what I would like to speak about," I say.

"Very well. On this occasion I will allow it as my husband is currently attending Divine Council. I could do with the distraction."

She turns and proceeds down the hallway turning left, her wings fluttering with each step. I follow behind, jogging to keep up. We reach a courtyard filled with juniper trees, housed in large marble pots, surrounding the perimeter. A glorious strawberry tree fills the courtyard's centre. Its branches splay like an umbrella shading the garden benches underneath. Psyche takes her place on one of the benches. I follow her lead and sit opposite on the other.

"You may begin semi god Siriarna," she says plucking a plump strawberry from the tree.

I am relieved Eros is not currently in residence, it would have made for an awkward conversation if he was present. Taking a deep breath, I speak my truth, "I have been on a personal quest which has ended here. With you."

"Oh, how exciting," says Psyche licking her strawberry stained lips.

She really is the most beautiful god I have ever seen. No wonder mortals came to worship her on the Surface World.

I continue, staring her straight in the eyes, "My quest was to find my true heritage, my god parent—"

Psyche interrupts, "That is forbidden information."

"My case is different."

Psyche draws closer, "Well, do go on," she says with impatience.

"I sought out Goddess Eileithyia on the Surface World. She shared an ancient legend only she and one other knew... you. A legend of a mortal princess in love with a god. One who had a secret affair with Zeus, and then fell pregnant. She told me how the princess married her god and came to her immediately after the ceremony to birth her child. I am that child."

"No, it cannot be. I won't hear this nonsense. You are lying." Psyche responds, however, her face has drained of its lustre.

"I promise you, I speak the truth. I have so many questions mother."

"Do not call me that. If what you say is true, my child would be long passed. I want you to leave now."

Her wings start to flutter wildly. This conversation is not going well. Although I didn't have any expectations, I had hoped Psyche would be happy to know her child had survived, that she was special, and very much alive. How could I have been so naive? I frantically try to salvage this reunion.

Leaning forward I say, "I was frozen in time by the Fates and left for Eileithyia to shelter until the ribbons of Time could no longer hold me."

The movement has exposed my pendant, and I see Psyche spy it. Her body stiffens, and her eyes are wild, "Where did you get that pendant?"

I reply cautiously, "Eileithyia gave it to me. She said it belonged to me, Psyche." I say, not making the same mistake by calling her mother.

"It was mine you know. My mother gave it to me one mortal birthday. My sisters were so jealous. Their pendants, amber for Cidippe and emerald for Aglaura, were not surrounded in gold like mine. They said I was favoured because I was the youngest and prettiest sibling. Both my sisters made my life miserable, Aglaura particularly. When I announced I was to marry Eros, she became blinded with envy. She tried to sabotage my upcoming wedding, and it was she who let Zeus into my room. Granted, I could have asked him to leave, but Aglaura tricked me into thinking it was a rite of passage to becoming a god. I did not question her lie. And I did not become a god at that moment, instead I became pregnant.

"The shame of my naivety almost cost me my true love and destiny, but I hid the pregnancy, determined to absolve my mistake as soon as I could. And Eileithyia was happy to oblige."

"Oh Psyche, I'm so sorry."

A brief laugh escapes her lips, "Do not feel sorry for me, Siriarna. I had my vengeance."

"What happened to Aglaura?" I ask, my heart skipping a beat.

A wicked smile turns the corner of her mouth as she speaks, "I slipped a potion into her drink the night of my farewell celebration. By the following morning, Aglaura was left mute, never able to speak another lie."

The look in her eyes is distant and menacing, not at all what I expected. The flash of ominous nostalgia is soon replaced by a peaceful expression as Psyche is brought back to the present.

Even though disturbed by her past revelations, Psyche seems receptive, so I take this opportunity to ask the question I came to Mount Olympus hoping to propose, "I would really like to stay in the Sky Realm and spend some time with you." I say, fidgeting on my seat as I deliver the words. I can't bring myself to meet Psyche's eyes and I have wrapped my arms around my body like armour.

"I'd like that Siriarna. Why don't you return to Evolirium, collect your belongings and say your farewells. You can come back here, to me, when you're ready."

Tears well in my eyes, and I brush them away before they have a chance to escape. Psyche floats forward and embraces me in an awkward hug, "Everything is going to be as it should, Siriarna."

I return to the chariot with a sense of future hope. My immortality will be beside the woman who gave birth to me. My godly mother, the beautiful Goddess of the Soul.

I turn to wave as I board the chariot and see Eros appear beside his wife. "Who is this my love?" I hear him say.

Psyche's answer is a whisper, but a god's whisper is not quiet. "Absolutely no-one you have to worry about—"

The chariot takes flight before I hear the rest of her sentence. Whilst I find my mother's words a little disturbing, I push them to the back of my mind because I completely understand how hard it will be for her to relive her past mistake with Zeus. I know by the time I return to the Sky Realm, Psyche will have everything ready for me.

CHAPTER 24

Siriarna

Returning to Evolirium is bittersweet. From magic average when I first arrived to magic everything as I prepare myself to leave the realm. It truly is an evolution I could never have imagined, even in my wildest dreams. I'm still getting my head around the fact that I was frozen in time for centuries. Gods, I'm old. Gods, I'm a god. I snort laugh out loud.

"Very becoming."

Startled, I snap my head around quickly hands outstretched, ready to use my power to protect myself.

"Whoa, easy does it," says Roman taking a step backward.

"Roman." I say and throw my arms around his waist, burying my head in his shoulder.

He ruffles my hair in response, and I am suddenly thrown back into the past. And I like the memories that come with it.

"When did you get back?" he asks.

"Right this second."

Just like when I first arrived into this realm, the boy across the pathway is easy-going and cheeky. Despite this year's disruption to our friendship, I'm going to miss him.

"Are you okay? I've been worried, ever since you lost your magic and left for The Between."

The concern in his voice is touching and I realise how much I previously leaned on his companionship. "Everything is fine Roman, better than fine actually."

"I've really missed you. You seem the same, but different," he says tilting his head and scrutinizing me.

I roll my eyes and respond, "I'm definitely a better me," I wink playfully.

"When you came out of the Void, you were so distraught. Understandably. And choosing to move to The Between, well that really floored me if I'm completely honest. Was it awful there?"

"It was better than I imagined. It took me a long time to fill the hole in my soul my missing power triggered. But, on a positive note, I found a lifetime friend in Miriam."

His eyes widen, "Miriam. Oh my gods, poor Miriam," he says surprised by the mention of her name.

"She's fine Roman. She's built a good life in The Between. As good as you can have without magic." I say wistfully.

"Speaking of magic, Siriarna, how are you coping without yours?"

I think about sharing my status with him but now is not the right time. I have a few things to take care of first. "So much has changed. For now, know I'm fine. Great actually."

"We've got so much to catch up on. I know you're holding something back. I know you too well, sweet Siriarna," he says mocking me.

Of course, he's right. "Go and get ready for Graduation, dear Roman. I'll see you tonight," I say fluttering my eyelashes.

"Shall we walk together? I offer my chaperone services," he says with a cheeky lilt to his voice.

"No. I'll meet you there... later."

He reaches forward and draws me into a tight embrace, "Okay, see you there. And Siriarna, I'm glad you're back," he says before retreating to his hut.

Tonight's Graduation Party is the perfect farewell to my time on Evolirium, almost like the Fates have aligned my destiny. And I am going to make the most of it.

I take in one last sweeping view of my hut. When I peer into the bedroom, I shudder as the memories of that awful night come flooding back. My magic vibrates throughout my veins signalling that I am no longer powerless. I conjure a ball of electricity to my palms in reassurance, nonetheless. Immediately, I feel better. Strong. Resilient. Me. And I feel... happy.

******

It's dusk, not midnight. Still, it will have to do if I am to achieve everything I dream of before leaving this realm.

Outside my hut, I am greeted by the final departure of the sun, leaving deep crimson and sinister claret shades in its wake. An unsettled chill makes its way down my spine despite the warmth of the evening. *A warning, perhaps?*

I shrug the feeling away and walk the dormitory

pathways in my black mission uniform, careful to avoid the overhead lighting. The path light outside the hut I am headed for explodes by thought, leaving the immediate vicinity in shadows.

"What are you doing here?" Alexandraya demands after answering the door to my banging. If not for the minor quiver in her voice, I would say she handled the shock of seeing me well.

"I've come to speak with you," I declare, my voice as calm as the Zen River.

"This is no place for a powerless semi god," she smirks. Her long black hair flicks as she pivots, poised to shut the door in my face.

"Lucky for me." I smile, and step into her doorway.

Her brows crease. "I need to get ready for Graduation. I've no time to waste with you."

Ignoring her insult, I square my shoulders before speaking. "I'm not leaving until you admit what you did to me."

We are standing, staring at each other. A showdown of souls, neither of us moving an inch. Her emerald eyes boring into mine, my return stare steely and determined. Her normally beautiful face turns into a sinister snarl, her lips curl, and her nostrils flare. She takes a step past me and peers left and right down the pathways. Noticing the absence of light, she answers, her face inches from my own, "Yes, it was me. And I'd do it again in a heartbeat."

"Why?" My voice cracks ever so slightly, but my resolve stands firm.

"I can't believe you are so stupid. I wanted to go to the gods' dinner. It was *my* destiny and you stole it. But don't fret, everything is as it should be now." As an afterthought, she adds, "If you're still pining after Roman, by all means have him. I'm done with the charade anyway."

My eyelids are blinking uncontrollably. All that pain because she wanted to go to a dinner.

Sensing my shock, she continues to inflict verbal abuse, "Miriam was also a casualty of her own importance. I doubt she feels that way now." A wicked smile lifts the corner of her lips.

I absent-mindedly bite my tongue. The blood tastes metallic but it is more pleasing than the sour memory of Miriam's floating body.

She is grinning now, smug in her sense of victory. That condescending smirk is wiped off her face as her sightline is drawn to the electricity in my palms. "How did you get your power back?" she shrieks.

I aim my first strike at her legs, and she falls screaming. Quickly, I launch myself on top of her body and send a charge to her chest, rendering her near unconscious. Guilt briefly makes an appearance, but I continue with my plan—vengeance for both me and my dearest Miriam.

******

Alexandraya

I must say, my surprise is an understatement when I answer the door and find Siriarna standing there. And I do not like surprises. This one was bitterly disappointing.

When magic appears in her palms I am taken aback. After all, I striped her Propensity power myself. For our heavens above sake, that's why she left Evolirium in the first place.

Like slow motion, I see the electricity leave her hand. I know I should run, but the shock renders me motionless. She strikes and maims me. I'm sure the attack will leave a scar. And on Graduation no less. It's not the gratifying end to my Evolirium journey that I had hoped for. I start to scream for my no longer flawless skin, and because Siriarna's eyes are thunderous. I have grossly underestimated her. My cries are snuffed out when she sends me into an almost cardiac arrest.

I'd be lying if I said I wasn't scared. The look on her face was one I never expected from Basic Siriarna. I'm sure I saw her lips curl upwards as she sent me spiralling to the bottom of the Void.

I should probably reflect on the irony of my new situation, but jealousy weaves its icy fingers around my heart. How *did* she get her powers back?

As soon as I have composed myself, I will use the tracking device Hermes left for me. I've been wearing it around my neck in place of my signature emerald pendant, which I left by mistake in Roman's hut.

Tonight, after the Graduation Party, Hermes is going to sweep me off me feet and fly me back to the Sky Realm where we are to be married. I have succeeded in my personal mission to marry a god. My wedding present will be to banish Siriarna to the Surface World. Then I won't have to ever see her again. The muscles of my mouth turn into a triumphant grin.

I start to hum in the emptiness, enjoying my thoughts in the darkened space. I could use my Propensity to lighten the Void, however, I am used to tight dark places. My guide mother taught me to use my time alone locked in isolation to envisage a successful future; for my own good, of course. Right now, I am thankful for her training.

CHAPTER 25

Siriarna

Finally returning to my hut after acquainting Alexandraya with her new accommodations, I hurriedly open my wardrobe and scan through the contents until I locate the perfect outfit for tonight's celebrations—a finely woven gold mini dress that sparkles when it catches the light. It was a gift from Linus and Stefanie for my eighteenth birthday, and it is the most beautiful garment I own. *Perfect*.

I pull the dress over my head, fasten my amethyst halo pendant around my neck, and slip my feet into a pair of strappy gold heels. As a final touch, I release my hair from its ponytail and comb it into soft waves, tucking my bangs behind my ears to frame my face. No longer will I hide behind a self-made mask.

Celebrations are kicking off by the time I arrive. The Zen is filled with students dressed up, ready to commemorate the completion of their first-year milestone.

The Arena is a picture of graduation perfection. Propensity Tents are lined together opposite the candle lit river. A waterfall of mountain elixir sits in the centre and music echoes throughout the space. Groups of students are laughing, mingling, and drinking.

A flash appears across the night sky, drawing my attention skyward. I see Apollo riding in his new chariot, crafted for him in The Between. He draws his bow and shoots an arrow over the Zen before soaring away, leaving thousands of tiny gold stars sprinkled in suspension over Evolirium. Deafening cheers erupt from the crowd as they spy the god and his gift. The mood is electrified, and my body responds with a gentle vibration coursing through my veins.

"Hey, you made it." I hear Roman say from behind.

I spin around, happy to see my friend. "Of course. I wouldn't miss it." I smile. "What's in your hand?" I ask noticing his fist clenched into a ball.

"Alexandraya's pendant. She left it at my hut. I haven't been able to find her tonight to return it," he says opening his hand.

I cast my eyes to his palm and examine the emerald pendant. A small gasp escapes from my lips, and my hand flies to my neck. The two are identical, with the exception of the gold surrounding my own. It's Psyche's sister Aglaura's pendant. I do my best to remain unaffected when I reply, "I'm sure she'll turn up."

His eyebrows raise quizzically, but before he can question my lie, Davina approaches.

"Hey Roman, have you seen Alexandraya?" she asks, Melodie sidling up behind her.

"Siriarna, what are you doing here?" Melodie says, the colour draining from her face as she recognises me.

"Just here to celebrate. I'll leave you to it." I reply before briskly walking away.

Her reaction verifies her involvement in my Void ordeal. Deep down, I knew all TON members were responsible—I will deal with her and Davina later. Right now, I have other plans. I refuse to let them ruin my night.

*****

I catch sight of Braxton by the river, and my heart skips a beat. He looks mysterious and sexy, dressed head to toe in black, his chestnut eyes captivating as I approach.

"I was hoping to see you again," he drawls, and instantly my heartbeat accelerates. Then he whispers in my ear, "You look gorgeous, by the way."

My cheeks heat at the compliment, and a thrilling shiver makes its way down my spine. I know it's time. "I think we should go somewhere more private to catch up."

"Sounds perfect," he says not breaking my gaze.

Boldly, I reach for his hand and lead him from the Zen, down the pathway, and into the meadow, which is deserted due to the celebrations. The fields are filled with moonflowers and evening primrose blooming under the night sky, their scent potent and romantic. Tonight, the whole space is breathtaking, lit up by Apollo's canopy of glittering stars. The gold of my dress catches the light and is shimmering, casting an ethereal glow.

Braxton takes my hand and leads me to a patch of clover-covered ground at the far end of the field. Here we sit, so close, almost but not quite touching. "I've missed you, Siriarna. Very much," he whispers, his face only inches from mine, the warmth of his breath lightly brushing my skin.

"I've missed you too, Braxton. It feels like I've been gone a lifetime."

He reaches forward and cups my face in his palms. Then he bends down and slowly kisses my lips ever so gently, angelic almost. My stomach flutters like a thousand butterflies trying to escape and my cheeks flush with anticipation. Encouraged by my body's response, Braxton takes off his shirt, rolls it up and places it on the clover before lowering my head backward onto the soft material. He is perched above me now and I pull his half naked body closer to mine, trailing my fingers over his muscles pausing as I discover a long scythe tattoo burned into the hard lines of his torso. He presses his mouth to mine, more urgently this time in the most intoxicating kiss I have ever experienced. I gently push him off while I half sit, reaching the hem of my dress and pulling it over my head, leaving me bare except for my underwear.

"Oh my Gods Siriarna, you are so beautiful. Are you sure you want to do this?"

I silence him with my lips on his, murmuring, "Yes,"

breathlessly.

Braxton's tongue is tracing the outline of my lips before it finds mine. When it does, they dance together to a beat so fervent, it's exhilarating. I rip at the last of my clothing while catching my breath as he does the same. I feel him against my thigh, skin on skin and shudder. He looks into my eyes questioningly and I smile, raising my hips in encouragement. He rolls on protection before gently entering my body. The most wondrous warmth floods my insides. We are moving together in unison, slowly at first until the passion takes hold and the movement becomes more urgent. My breathing becomes rapid and I cling to his flesh, guided by his rhythm. Under the golden starlit sky, in the headily fragrant meadow, I cry out as my body fills with heat and explodes into the most exquisite pleasure I have ever known.

My heart is filled with pure joy. I want this night to last forever. A thousand sensations course through my body at the same time. Elation, wonder, tenderness—I can't put the emotions into words. I feel like a goddess and not in the literal sense of the word. The symbolic nature of Braxton's scythe tattoo, the epitome of perfection—time.

Time to heal. Time to live. Time to love.

I nestle into the crook of his arm and allow myself to fall into a blissful sleep.

I am soon jarred awake by Braxton's sudden flinch. He frantically points to the sky above, and I see a flaming ball of energy heading directly toward us at speed. It's going to make contact any second, of that I am certain. I also know we need time to stop it before it connects with our realm.

My eyes sweep over his face one last time, then I whisper to him, "Braxton, you need to turn back Time."

He looks at me and howls, "You won't remember."

"I know." And a piece of my heart tears beneath my ribs. "Help me remember," I say, a tear sliding down my cheek.

... Time to forget.

*****

Braxton

I can't believe we're here together in the meadow, alone. It's what I've been praying to the Fates for. Watching her sleep in my arms is the final crescendo, and I sigh with satisfaction, staring up at the golden stars left behind by

Apollo.

I see it first, hurtling toward Evolirium at breakneck speed. A ball flaming so bright, it's hard to miss. I jerk upright causing Siriarna to wake and now she sees it too. Our realm will be no longer if the energy ball makes contact. That I am sure of.

Taking in the menacing phenomena lighting the sky, she looks up at me and asks me to turn back time.

It's closing in and I know she's right. I don't want to do it, I don't want her to forget this perfect moment, but in my soul I know I have no choice. With my heart hammering, breaking, ripping from of my chest, I summon the ribbons of Time to my palm.

Then I twist.

CHAPTER 26

Siriarna

I've just left Roman and I'm standing near the Zen River. A strange feeling of déjà vu pricks at the corner of my mind. Pushing it aside, I smooth down my golden dress and scan the Zen. Braxton is rushing toward me, "Hi," I say showcasing my biggest smile, "I was hoping to find you here."

His forehead is creased and his eyes are bleak, "Listen, Siriarna, there's something I need to tell you... there is a ball of energy on its way to Evolirium right now and we have to stop it. Otherwise, it will likely destroy our realm," he says urgently.

I have no idea what he's talking about. This is

definitely not what I had pictured for our reunion after months of being apart. "I don't understand," I say shaking my head. "How do you know this?"

"I have seen it before. I had to turn back time," he says grabbing my arm. "We have to hurry to the meadow. There's not much time."

I knew something felt different, the time shift explains my earlier uneasiness. My legs are heavy as we trudge forward, my heartbeat frantic at the thought of this precious realm in danger.

Roman is on the grassy mounds as we approach. He starts to speak, but Braxton ignores him forging onward. He follows behind anyway.

Now in the meadow, Braxton points to Evolirium's atmosphere. There's nothing there and I'm beginning to question his sanity.

"What's going on Braxton?" Roman says as confused as I am.

"There," Braxton points.

Now I see it. It's just a spec of light in the far distance, but it's moving at a remarkable pace.

"Oh my gods," Roman says as he spies it too.

I have to think, and quickly. Will my power be enough

to stop the impact? Neither Braxton nor Roman know of my abilities. "I'm going to need your help. Both of you." I voice matter-of-factly.

Two questioning stares are aimed at me, but no verbal response follows; my tone yielding the desired no-time-to-explain effect.

"When I give the order, Braxton, I want you to slow time without stopping it completely. We can't let the object get too close or the explosion from impact will still cause devastation to the realm." I direct. "Roman, I'm going to need you to send my power to the target at the speed of light. If we work together, we can stop this."

Thankfully, my speech comes across more positive than the way I truly feel about this last minute, and highly rushed, plan. It's possible we'll die trying, but we are at the mercy of time. And we are the only ones in the realm who know of the imminent threat.

Please help us. I silently pray to the Fates.

Roman speaks out, "I don't understand, Siriarna. What are you talking about?"

Settling my eyes firmly onto his, I say, "There's no time to explain. Trust me."

He nods.

I switch my gaze to Braxton, draw in a deep breath and stand firm, "Now, Braxton." I yell.

He does as instructed, conjuring the ribbons of Time to his palm. Then he expertly twists the cord to slow Evolirium's rhythm. His Propensity power is impressive. However, I notice his clenched jaw and reddening skin tone. Time to strike.

Summoning the largest ball of electricity I can create to my palm, I release it with every ounce of force I can evoke. "Now, Roman." I shout.

Roman engulfs my electricity with Light and sends the electromagnetic waves toward the target at light speed as Braxton releases Time. It hits the energy ball with a fortunate stroke of serendipity. All that is left of the menacing object is a firework of scattered fragments illuminating the sky. A beautiful and mesmerising averted catastrophe.

"We did it." Roman says pulling me into a hug.

Braxton shoots an icy stare in his direction. "How did you get your magic back?" he asks me in a softer tone than his expression portrays.

I disengage from Roman, who also raises an eyebrow. Before I have time to explain my immortality, a chariot descends into the meadow, led by two golden maned extraordinary immortal horses.

Apollo throws a matching golden ladder over the side. "Roman, Siriarna, come with me. Now."

The ever smooth and youthful facial appearance of the Great God is tarnished with a scowl. In stark contrast, Roman is beaming. He has always openly displayed his admiration for Apollo. Without hesitation, he is leaping into the chariot. I, on the other hand, am a little wary. How can I leave the realm that was almost destroyed? However, the seriousness of Apollo's expression leads me gradually toward the transport.

Braxton grabs my arm, and the previous feeling of déjà vu resurfaces. "Siriarna, please don't go," he pleads. The look in his eyes is melancholic. Behind the sadness I glimpse a desperation in his widened chestnut eyes. "I'll be back soon, don't worry." I say climbing the rungs of the ladder.

My last thought, however, is Alexandraya tucked away in the not-so-comfort of the Void. My conscience settles as I make a mental note to return in three days to release my cousin.

******

Apollo

I catch Siriarna as she faints following the revelation that the strike was meant for her. That's when I realise I cannot disclose who launched the attack. Not yet.

The Fates have shared her parentage with me in a premonition. As the truth was unveiled, I found myself in complete shock—that is a rare occurrence in my line of abilities. My purpose is clear. This tiny god will be under my protection and my protection will be paramount. Once her ancestry is revealed to the heavens, there will be turbulent times ahead. Battle lines will be drawn and danger will follow. I'm ready though, ready to guard her with all of my being.

Peering into her pale violet eyes just now, my own immortality reflected back at me, proves this is where I belong. Here, by Siriarna's side.

Even if I didn't want to, I would heed the Fates' request. Otherwise, I could face the punishment Eileithyia was bestowed—entombment in her cave on Knossos for all eternity. The Fates reacted severely for breaking their most coveted law in revealing Siriarna's ancestry to her person. I'm lucky I don't have to fight my destiny, I *want* to be part of Siriarna's life. I *need* to for I relish the destiny I have foreseen.

Bringing Roman along was a last minute decision. How could I leave my son in a realm that is under attack?

CHAPTER 27

Siriarna

I am temporarily stunned by Apollo's revelation that the attack bound for Evolirium was meant for me. So much so, the air leaves my body and I fall limp toward the chariot floor. Luckily Apollo is as quick as he is gifted, and I regain consciousness moments later in his arms.

Now upright, and with the Progression Realm fast becoming a distant image, I turn him and ask, "Who is hunting me?"

His expression is stiff, and it's clear he doesn't want to disclose the information he holds. I ask again, "Apollo, I need to know. Now." I say forcefully.

He lets out a deep sigh, then responds, "Your mother

is trying to erase your existence."

"But... but I just saw her and she... oh, right." I finish mid question as I realise exactly why Psyche wants me gone. She wants her secret buried, for the second time in history. Only this time, she wants to ensure it's permanent.

I scream into the open air, then let out a guttural cry as I realise the future I longed to embrace, has been ripped from my soul.

Roman throws a protective arm around my shoulder steadying my swaying body. "You know who your mother is?" he utters baffled.

I start to hyperventilate as my thoughts return to Psyche. I can't say her name out loud. I can't tell Roman the discovery of my past. I'm ashamed I was foolish enough to believe my future was going to be alongside *her.*

"Take it easy Siriarna, we're almost there." Apollo says.

I'm lost in a surge of emotions. The rhythm of the horses gentle yet steady rocking movements, combined with Roman's grip, provide an unspoken solace.

Within moments, we've exited the vortex and I am again passing through the golden gates of Mount Olympus. Instead of recoiling at the thought of re-entering the Sky Realm, I know exactly what I need to do.

And I hope I don't cause a war by doing so. Actually, I don't really care if I do.

The horses come to rest outside a modest looking palace, quite the contrast to Psyche's. Just the thought of her makes my head spin, and I steady myself by gripping the chariot rail. Apollo throws down the golden ladder from the chariot door while stepping from the carriage himself. Roman, follows, leaping from the chariot and offering his hand. Gratefully I take it as I climb down the ladder in my golden graduation dress and strappy heels.

Inside Apollo's living room, I spy a jug of nectar on the table and immediately pour myself a glass, guzzling it in one smooth gulp. I had hoped my first taste of the divine liquid would have been in more pleasing circumstances. Barely, I manage to take in the heady mix of aroma and flavour, but the sensation falls flat.

"Whoa, slow down, Nectar is not something to be messed with. Especially, if you are not used to its effects." Apollo warns.

Roman moves forward and looks me squarely in the eyes. "I think you should listen to Apollo, Siriarna," he says with an authoritarian tone.

Like he would ever disagree with his favourite god.

"Duly noted." I smirk sarcastically refilling my glass and chugging down my second drink.

Shoving Roman out of the way, I approach Apollo. "Tell me how you came to know my history and my mother's plan to erase my existence." The query is bold, the nectar taking effect, giving me a sense of bravado.

Apollo obliges my request through raised eyebrows, "I have precognition abilities linking me directly to the Fates." He discloses. "They have revealed your past, your present and your intended future."

Roman's jaw drops at the admission and he lets out an impressed gasp. Could he love his hero anymore? Highly doubtful.

I have always been in awe of the Fates and their binding authority on the destiny of humankind. Knowing Apollo has a direct linkage to them, makes me shudder. And the fact that he is aware of my future, is unnerving.

"Eileithyia told me they spared my life and kept me frozen, bound by the ribbons of Time until they could no longer hold." I divulge. Thinking of Eileithyia warms my heart and makes me want to run straight to her comfort, like the shielded blanket I need right now. "Perhaps I should go and visit her."

Roman stares at me, clearly taken aback by this unexpected disclosure about my past. He looks like he's about to say something, perhaps to ask me again who my god parent is, but Apollo speaks first.

"I'm sorry to be the barer of bad news Siriarna, but Eileithyia has been entombed in her cave, bound to solitary for all eternity."

"Oh my gods, no. No. Why?" I ask horrified.

Eileithyia relishes her role as midwife and overseer of pregnancy and life. This will surely destroy her soul. I start to sob, soft tears becoming a steady and unstoppable stream.

"She committed the ultimate betrayal by sharing what was forbidden. She is lucky the Fates did not commit her to the Furies." Apollo answers frowning.

It's too much. My head is swimming with memories of the god who sacrificed her own happiness to provide me with the answers I needed. A truly selfless act, knowing she would be risking her future. I can't control my tears. I cry and cry, my body heaving with each sob.

Both Apollo and Roman stand by allowing me to grieve, not saying a word as I fill my third glass of Nectar and gulp. I want to numb the pain. So much pain. My god mother trying to harm me, and the god who cared enough for me, to put me before her. Two completely opposite intentions. Each characteristic cutting wounds deep into my soul.

I want to confront Psyche now, I want her to suffer as I am. Standing, I attempt to retreat from Apollo's palace. He reaches out and grips my arm, anticipating my response, and attempting to stop me from leaving. I thrash my head about in protest of Apollo's strong hold, but the nectar is swirling through my head and the dizziness returns with a vengeance. I stumble backwards into Roman who instantly wraps his arms around me in a tight clinch, and I reluctantly loll my head against his chest.

"Everything will be fine," Roman says releasing me from his embrace.

I don't agree with his statement, everything has gone so incredibly wrong.

"I think it best you sleep off the nectar." Apollo suggests.

Twisting my hair around my fingers so tightly, almost severing it at the roots, I debate continuing my reckless plight. But my body is suddenly wracked with a strange buzzing. My thoughts are flying out of my mind and I reach out to touch them. Of course, there's nothing there and I fall, this time making contact with the marble floor. Perhaps it hurts. I can't tell. My entire being is numb from both the nectar and the staggeringly soul crushing revelations.

"Time to rest, Siriarna."

As my head hits a pillow, I hear the distant voices of Roman and Apollo before the click of a door, darkness immediately replacing light.

Just like the depths of my soul.

******

I wake sometime in the early morning hours, darkness still blanketing the realm, but the murmurs of daylight indicate the break of dawn is imminent. I instantly raise my hands to my temple. Perhaps I should have listened to Apollo's warnings about the nectar. However, the pain masks the incessant gnawing madness that has taken residence in my heart.

I wish I had something other than my golden dress to

wear, it seems inappropriate in the circumstances. But as I smooth my hands over the material, the origin of the dress immediately comes to mind—Stefanie and Linus. My so much more than guide parents. A renewed sense of love hits me as I envisage my dress as much needed armour. As a final touch I slick my hair back into a ponytail, securing it with a sliver of ripped bed sheet. I'm ready.

It's time.

Creeping from the palace, I make my way to Apollo's chariot. My nerves start to fray and I quash them with a sharp intake and exhale of breath. This not the reunion I had envisaged.

You stole my dream, Psyche and I will not go down without a fight.

The horses are wide awake, sensing the new day is almost upon us. I ruffle their manes. They really are magnificent specimens, and I am rewarded with unison whinnies, the equines unaware of the calamitous circumstances surrounding this morning's journey. I whisper my instructions to both Lampos and Actaeon and the horses take flight.

May the Fates have mercy on my soul.

It's a rocky start, the horses not accustomed to their temporary mistress, but we manage to arrive at the opposite side of the realm unscathed. My mood is now as black as the storm clouds that have coincidentally just appeared.

Throwing the ladder over the side of the chariot, I hurtle down the rungs, running toward my mother's door screaming her name... "PSYCHE."

There is no response. I pound my fists on her door and wait. Still nothing. Bringing electricity to my palms, I release the full force of my power at the door. Fragments of timber splinter throughout the entryway of the elaborately carved palace.

Stepping over the debris, I charge through the empty spaces, gaining momentum until I'm sprinting from room to room, searching for Psyche. I'm still screaming her name, but the echoes fade into the empty voids, unheard. Out of breath, I slow down and find myself at the courtyard where I sat with her and revealed she was my mother. Fury engulfs me. I send my electricity to the strawberry tree, striking it down. The plump fruit strewn lifeless, leaving a blood-like stain on the previously pristine marble.

I return to the chariot spent and manic. The familiar sensation of burning pierces the sockets behind my eyes. Glaring at the cumulonimbus above, the clouds respond with thunderous rumbles. Pelting rain soon follows, furiously thrashing the earth beneath—a testament to my growing wrath. The hefty drops shower the realm around me, everywhere except in my direct vicinity.

My mind is abuzz, but it zeros in on the only choice my mother's absence has left me. I hoist myself into the chariot, Grand Palace bound.

CHAPTER 28

Siriarna

The horses are agitated by the storm, making it difficult to control the chariot. Thankfully, the clear bubble around me remains, ensuring safe passage to my destination. The home of my unknowing father.

Well not for long.

I climb down the chariot ladder one rung at a time, my resolute hardening with each step. By the time I reach the ground I am poised, ready to reveal the centuries-kept secret of my parentage. With my newly calm resolve, the clouds dissipate and the sky is returned to its former tranquil conditions.

I beat my fists against the imposing entrance doors to

the Grand Palace and stand firm. After a second round of banging, the door is answered by Hera.

"Who are you?" Demands the Queen of Mount Olympus.

Hera is every bit as forthright as her fabled reputation. Raising my eyes to hers, I step forward and introduce myself, "I am Siriarna, and I need to speak with Zeus immediately."

Hera scans my face with intrigue before answering, "He's at the Council Arena, preparing for this afternoon's wedding. I could escort you, but I need a word with my husband."

"No need, I'm sure I'll find it." I swiftly turn on my high heel backing away.

I hear the angry slam of doors behind me. According to legend, Hera does not like being excluded from affairs of the Sky Realm, especially those involving her husband. She senses something is brewing, the previous state of the horizon, a mighty indication. I don't have much time. Hera's feelings regarding Zeus' illegitimate children are well known throughout the realms. This wound will cut deeply. It seems my immortality will not bring the peace I crave.

After a quick canter, the horses now comfortable with my command, we halt at an open circular arena surrounded by 12 carved columns shaped as statues of the Olympian Gods. At the upper end, sits an elaborately sculptured throne directly in front of Zeus' statue and my father is currently standing behind it, surveying the empty space.

The grandeur of the Council Arena is stately and powerful. The illustrations we studied on Evolirium were an exact replica but on paper, did not show the true glory I sight in person. I instantly understand why it is the perfect setting for a godly wedding. *Will my mother be there?*

"What are you doing here semi god?" Zeus thunders as he catches sight of me.

I step forward, shadowed by the scale of the space, however, no longer in hiding. I am here to speak my truth and I pray to the Fates my father takes the news of my godly bloodline, his bloodline, well. The nerves start to tingle through my veins and settle into knots within my stomach. For a moment, my resolve weakens, but then I think of Psyche and what lengths she was willing to take to keep her secret buried. Clearing my throat, I say, "My name is Siriarna, and I am your daughter." No nonsense, no stuttering, just the facts of his involvement in giving me life.

His posture remains stout, his head steady, but his steel grey eyes are widened, and I see the storm brewing behind them. He takes a step forward and I am plunged further into darkness by his shadow. This imposing god, the Almighty Zeus, is towering above me shaking his head. "Impossible," he says through gritted teeth. However, as he bends to my level, he gazes into my eyes and I know he feels what I do. An instant kindred.

He sways backward and unwittingly seats himself into his throne. "Who is your mother?" he asks while smoothing his long thick beard.

Without hesitating, I answer... "Psyche."

The confusion is clear as his brows knit together. Then a knowing nod replaces the emotion as he delves deep into his long ago past. "On Knossos."

"Yes." I answer.

"I'm not sure I understand," he says firmly, trying to link the centuries ago past to my 18 year old self standing in front of him now.

"The Fates suspended and bound me to the ribbons of

Time until Time could no longer hold me. I was guarded by Eileithyia." My soul weeps at the mention of the goddess' name.

"Eileithyia? She should have come to me. We have no secrets," he declares, although his face displays the contradiction.

Before another word is spoken, Hera arrives. The arena suddenly feels small and suffocating. "There you are." She directs her question to Zeus. "Hermes is looking for you, he needs to go over last minute wedding details."

He scratches his head, looks to me, and then to his wife. "Come to my palace after the wedding, Siriarna. We have much to discuss," he says before disappearing in a silver flash.

"I guess it's just the two of us, again." Hera says crisply. "A warning to the wise—and I hope you are, Siriarna. Go back to Evolirium where you belong. Stay out of the Sky Realm, there is no business here for you." She disappears, just as quickly as her husband.

Countless tumultuous thoughts of the day's events are crashing through my mind, like a tidal wave waiting to swallow me whole. I stare to the clouds above and hear their rumble at my thought. My power is growing. I know who I am. I will not be silenced nor discarded.

Catching the reflection of my golden dress in the marble column beside me, the statue of Apollo no less, I decide it will be the perfect outfit to attend a wedding. And a huge smile spreads across my face.

CHAPTER 29

Alexandraya

Hermes was concerned when he rescued me from the Void. I let him think he was my true saviour and played the victim well. I almost feel sorry for Siriarna. Hermes will show no mercy when the time comes. My eternally youthful looking future husband. I snuggle closer to his chest as we make our journey to the Sky Realm.

My feet barely touch the smooth marble ground of Mount Olympus before I am whisked away to one of the grand sitting rooms. Nymphs have been called in to help with my wedding preparations and they are fussing around, making sure everything is perfect for the ceremony.

A bath is drawn in the eccentric golden powder room, filled with bay laurel leaf infused water, and scented in lavender. Pots of oils surround the tub and will be massaged into my skin. Elder flower tea is served, and the bathing ritual is about to begin. It is exactly what I need to wash the memory of Evolirium from my mind. My future lies here, in this heavenly realm.

"I see your ritual is about to begin. I wish I could join you in it," Hermes says mischievously, entering the room.

"My love, if only you could," I reply seductively, my thoughts returning to the present.

Horrified nymphs scatter to throw Hermes out of the room, stating it is bad luck for the groom to see the bride before the ceremony. I simply throw back my head and laugh as Hermes blows me a kiss before the door is closed behind him. I have no belief in silly superstitions. I drop my clothing and step into the luxurious bath, starting the journey to my impending wedding, and subsequent transition into Goddess Alexandraya. I repeat those words in my head *Goddess Alexandraya*. I love the way that sounds.

*****

The chiton is slipped over my head, and I stand back to admire the dress in the floor length mirror. It is so much taller than the standard sized mirrors in any other realm. Of course, I look amazing. I twirl one way, then the other, gaining a complete view of myself in the reflection.

"You look incredible," a young nymph says.

It's true, I do look incredible. The chiton is made of light, pure white silk fabric clinging to my body like a second skin. The gown is sleeveless and fastens over my right shoulder with the material falling in soft folds to my ankles. A simple gold belt cinches my tiny waist. The whole look is sexy and elegant, exactly how I had hoped. Another nymph finishes styling my hair into long cascading ringlets and a deep red stain is applied to my lips. As a final touch, I slip my feet into a pair of stilettos, to elongate my semi god height. I am ready to go. Looking back in the mirror, I wonder how tall I will end up once my transition is completed. I smile at my reflection, knowing I will look even more amazing as Goddess Alexandraya. The thought brings a natural crimson flush to my cheeks.

This is it. I take my place at the entrance of the Council

Arena. The space is filled with a private consortium of gods. I will surprise my guide parents after the wedding, turning up in the Home Realm transition completed. Julienne, particularly, will be proud I fulfilled my destiny—the one she instilled should be mine from the minute I was placed in her arms.

I see Zeus standing beside Hermes at the opposite end of the runway on the purpose built alter, Hera at his side. I recognise some of the other gods from the dinner I attended, but there are many faces I have never seen in person before. That will change once I take up residence in Hermes' palace. *My* palace! I plan on throwing lots of housewarming parties including those gods who didn't make Hermes list of attendees today. I can hardly contain my delight.

My only regret is that Davina and Melodie could not be here today. Their compliance and loyalty over the years has been infallible. Replacing these loyal maidens will be a chore, however, I believe I will find worthy allies in time. And my time will soon be infinite. I should have been born a god, but the Fates had other ideas. They, obviously, wanted me to prove myself worthy. And that I have done. I can't help but wonder what gift of power they will bestow.

My eyes mist over as I scan the offerings of jewellery, gold and other exotic trinkets lining the flower-trimmed walkway. With more excitement than I can bear, I am ready to start my journey toward my soon-to-be husband and the rest of my eternal life.

How fortuitous that Psyche is walking me down the aisle. I knew I was of royal blood. *Knew it!* When she came forward and told me of my ancient past connection to her family, it was like kismet. Her beauty is insurmountable. I am quite in awe of this goddess, my own distant relation. The irony is not lost on me.

I pause for effect to scan the crowd, producing my best smile as I make eye contact with my immortal guests. The gasp from the crowd only justifies my efforts leading up to this moment were worth it. Feeling on top of the realm, I take my first steps.

That's when I see *her.*

I absolutely cannot for the life of me, believe what I am seeing. Siriarna!

CHAPTER 30

Siriarna

When I set down Lampos and Acteon outside Apollo's Palace, both he and Roman are waiting and neither look happy to see me, scowls creasing their foreheads.

Roman has changed out of his graduation clothing and is wearing one of Apollo's robes, which surprisingly fits, a little big, but nowhere near as oversized as I would have expected. In fact, looking from semi god to god, I notice they share the same sandy golden locks and piercing pale blue eyes. "Where have you been? I've been sick with worry," he chastises.

"I've been on a mission of self-discovery." I answer, however, my gaze is set on Apollo.

He nods as I knew he would. After all, he has seen my future. Initially, this bothered me but as I come to terms with all that I am, I find the thought comforting.

"We have a wedding to get to. Apollo is taking me as his guest." Roman says trying, but failing to hide his euphoria. This dalliance in the Sky Realm really suits him. He looks good here. Comfortable and at ease.

"I think I'll join you two."

"I thought semi gods were forbidden to attend a higher ceremony without invitation," he looks at me sceptically, then to Apollo, who nods his agreeance at the change of plan.

"It's okay Roman. I'm exactly where I'm meant to be."

My cryptic response is met with raised eyebrows but he does not push the point any further.

If I'm honest, I'm hoping Psyche will be amongst the guests. We have unfinished business. Perhaps a wedding is not the best place to have the necessary confrontation, but my mother did try to erase my existence, so I doubt there'll ever be a right time. And after my meeting with Zeus going better than expected, I am poised, ready for a familial battle. Just to be safe, I silently ask the Fates to smooth the pathway ahead.

******

Apollo's horses let out a familiar neigh as I board the chariot yet again. Although this time, I will not take charge of the reins. Instead, I gaze abstractedly at the horizon once airborne, and try to prepare for the unknown. A light gust of wind kisses my skin cooling my temperament—a reminder to stand strong. *A message from the Fates?*

With Apollo at the helm and out of earshot, Roman whispers, "Siriarna, I know that faraway look. I'm worried you're going to do something irrational."

Ever perceptive, is my dear friend. If only he knew how true that statement could end up. If my mother is at the ceremony, I'm not even sure of the consequences myself. "Hmm." I respond vaguely.

Luckily, he doesn't press me any further. The Council Arena spectacular shifts his focus.

"Wow," he whistles as we pull up at the ceremony. "This is something else."

I agree, the whole space has been completely transformed. Flowers fill the Arena providing a picturesque sight and a heavenly fragrance. It reminds me of Stefanie's masquerade parties. Only this time, I am not hiding behind a mask.

I scan the small gathering of gods in the arena but do not find my mother amongst them.

Standing at the end of the aisle is Hermes, flanked by Zeus and Hera. I wonder who has caught the attention of the great messenger. Hermes has been declared a play-god and one who is happy that his reputation precedes him. I am eager to meet his bride. *Maybe, when I take my place here in the Sky Realm, the two of us will be friends.*

I have rejected Hera's warning. I belong in this realm, it is my birthright, and I will take what is rightfully mine. For the sake of myself, and the sacrifice of Eileithyia. And above all, despite Psyche.

Apollo guides both Roman and me to the front of the ceremony, a place where we are not overshadowed. I am again, reunited with my father but it is not his eyes that I am drawn to. Hera is casting an icy stare in my direction. *She knows.* My body stiffens at the visual interrogation.

Roman's hand claps mine and he squeezes it gently. "Everything okay?" he asks in response to my rigid posture.

I don't trust myself to speak, so I nod instead. All the while searching the ceremony guests for my mother, who remains absent.

Zeus clears his throat, "The Ceremony shall begin," he announces. And all divine attendees turn to face the Arena entrance.

"Oh My Gods," Roman speaks out loud as he spies the bride.

Apollo instantly moves to my side and places a hand on my shoulder, "Siriarna—"

He tries to drag me from the Arena but I step into the aisle in defiance. My breath instantly catches in my throat, and the deafening thud of my heartbeat fills my ears.

Alexandraya is dressed in white. And my mother is standing by her side.

Merciless thoughts enter my mind. I can't stop them and I don't want to. The sky turns from its heavenly blessing, dotted with fluffy white clouds, to an ominous and threatening black.

Alexandraya shrieks as her eyes scan the Arena finding both Roman and myself in front of the temporary alter. Psyche, following her gaze, looks at me, then Zeus and turns to flee.

Don't you dare, Mother.

That's when all the rage pent up inside my veins is released skyward. The atmosphere growls in response. The previous gentle breeze transforms into an ear piercing blustery howl, and the clouds charge like a giant battery in the sky. A downpour of torrential raindrops smashes into the arena. Flowers are ripped apart, petals strewn lifeless throughout the space. The intensity of the thunderstorm is gathering momentum with each ragged breath that I release.

"Stop, Siriarna." Roman begs as he realises my power is responsible.

All I hear is my heartbeat.

Apollo places one hand on each of my shoulders, trying to break my concentration with the cumulonimbus, but my mind stands strong in unison with the clouds.

A lightning bolt flies from the sky and strikes Psyche's robes, pinning her in place, a weathered shackle. Her brilliant sapphire eyes are widened and scared. *Good.*

Alexandraya, dives from the strike and into the arms of Hermes who wraps her to him protectively.

I witness the hurt spread over Roman's face and my

heart lurches—thunder rumbles from the sky in response.

This storm is now out of control. The small cluster of gods at the ceremony are shielding themselves with their power but the electrical storm is gaining traction.

Hera yells to Zeus to put an end to the menace.

Instead of stopping the attack himself, Zeus steps forward and takes my hands in his. "Slow your mind, child. Close your eyes," he says gently. An instruction from master to apprentice.

As my eyelids shut, my sight to the skies above is obstructed. My erratic breathing begins to subside, soon returning to its normal beat. The clouds respond to my body's rhythm and revert to their previous wispy state in a peaceful cerulean sky.

A collective sigh of relief reverberates around the Arena, but an inquisitive awe settles in its place. I have demonstrated my power, and my bloodline, in front of the Olympian Gods.

"There will be no wedding today." My father decrees as the spectacle dies down.

"No. Please no." Alexandraya sobs amongst her confusion over the power I wielded.

Psyche, still pinned in position, has her attention

focused on Hera. I witness a look pass between them that confuses me.

Zeus releases my mother and beckons her forward. Once Psyche is standing by his side, he says, "I think it's time we acknowledge the child we conceived."

There's that look again between my father's wife and my mother.

"What?!" Alexandraya says horrified.

Roman casts his eyes from Alexandraya to me. He looks at me like it's the first time he's really seen me. Seen beneath the shy, awkward exterior.

Zeus formally addresses the crowd, "I would like to introduce you all to Siriarna, Goddess of Above."

CHAPTER 31

Alexandraya

No. Oh my gods, no. What is going on? My head is spinning. Siriarna is here at my wedding on Mount Olympus. How did this happen? She's not invited. She's a nobody. And why has Psyche dug her nails into my arm at the sight of her. How does she know Siriarna?

Just when I thought seeing Siriarna was the worst thing that could happen, I spy Roman standing next to her. He's here, at my wedding. Now this could get awkward. He was the perfect pawn in my game of godly chess. He served his purpose and was supposed to remain on Evolirium. I knew he'd be a little heartbroken at my disappearance from the realm, and without explanation no less. But all wars have casualties, even personal ones. Unfortunately, he was in the crossfire. I hope he's not going to cause a problem. I don't need an angry ex to wreak havoc with my carefully laid plans. Surely he knows he's not part of my future. I mean, for gods' sake I'm in a wedding dress, and he's not the one standing at the end of the aisle.

Clouds have suddenly turned threatening above the Council Arena replacing the heavenly skies of mere moments ago. My beautiful day is turning thunderous, like my former glorious mood.

The sound of the wind is terrifying and the rainfall is violent. No—my beautiful wedding—my flowers—my dress! The whole place is being destroyed.

Oh my gods' it's Siriarna! She's causing the destruction. How is she wielding this power?

Zeus steps in and controls the situation. Of course he does, he's the Ruler of all Gods and this catastrophic interruption is unacceptable. The skies clear and I'm ready to continue my wedding. After all, that is the reason we're here. Regardless of my uninvited and unwanted guests, I want to marry Hermes and transition into the goddess I deserve to be.

WHAT. NO. NO. NO.

Siriarna is Zeus and Psyche's daughter. How? I can't make sense of this. Yet strangely, it makes total sense. Perhaps that's because we're related. That detail has left an icy finger clawing at my soul.

My wedding has been delayed. Destroyed by the very person I have despised since the moment I met her. I take a deep breath and remind myself this is temporary.

I hate her. I hate her more than I ever have.

I will have my vengeance.

******

Roman

When Apollo invited me into his chariot after the almost disaster on Evolirium, I couldn't believe my luck. And why was Braxton left behind, not that I'm complaining. My most worshipped god inviting me to his palace, I couldn't board quick enough. And when he advised Siriarna's mother was responsible for the attack on Evolirium, I was gobsmacked. Turns out that was only the beginning of my bewilderment. Perhaps I should never have accepted Apollo's invitation. Although now I think about it, at the time it did seem to be more of a demand.

Siriarna handled the news of her pre-planned demise well. Although I guess the nectar helped, in part, overcome her immediate distress. It's not like her to take such extreme measures, stealing a chariot for example, but that is one of her many new found traits. Through the bravado, behind her violet eyes, I see she still needs reassurance. And I will always be there to offer it— 'Friends First Always'. I stand by that.

Attending a god's wedding is the icing on the ambrosia. It's not something a semi god would normally experience, so when Apollo offered me a place as his guest, I was both honoured and thrilled. Siriarna joining us on the momentous occasion, being the perfect ending to our time in the Sky Realm. I must say, I am going to miss this realm. But I am now more than determined than ever to study hard in Light Propensity, because I must become a member of The Core. Failing is not an option. I want to continue my close association with the gods of this realm and being in The Core will solidify my connection.

The ceremony is commencing and we all turn to welcome the bride. What? I don't believe it. It's

Alexandraya. In a wedding dress. She's the bride. It takes me a minute to register what is going on. She was missing from the Graduation Party, and then I was whisked away before I could search for her. Seems she had other plans. My heart heaves like it's being ripped from my chest, and I feel like such a fool. This semi god, my partner, is about to marry a god. How could I have been so stupid, how could I have competed? I've been played a fool, and I do not like it. Next to the pain, a wave of resentment finds residency at the centre of my soul.

Siriarna's body stiffens when she recognises Alexandraya. Then the most unexpected phenomenon occurs. The skies above have begun to attack the Arena. And Siriarna is responsible. Just who is her mother? And how is she wielding such power?

I beg her to stop, surely her safety is at risk? But it's no use. Zeus steps in and, like the mighty powerful ruler he is, takes control, guiding Siriarna to reign in her power.

My questions are soon answered by the King of Gods. Siriarna is the offspring of Zeus himself and the Goddess Psyche. Psyche who is attached to Alexandraya's arm. My mind is swirling with so many questions.

Looking at my best friend, I see the shift, I can't believe

I didn't before. She's extraordinary. Of course she is. Deep down, I guess I always knew it. She is quite literally glowing. Is that a faint golden halo circling her head?

I'm here for you Siriarna. Just like always.

******

Braxton

I am quite literally counting down the seconds until Siriarna returns. It's taking every inch of self-control not to speed time forward and have Siriarna here with me instantly. It's been days, but still I wait in the meadow. She said she would return, and I believe her.
In the meantime, I am stuck in the bleak, sunless merry-go-round that is my memory—a constant gnawing reminder of what I have lost.

I know the only way I will be able to continue is to somehow help Siriarna remember. Remember the night that changed my life, and hers. A time when everything was so right. I will beg, borrow and steal all the nectar I need to fulfil my promise. I won't give up until I succeed. For her sake and mine.

In the meantime, I wrap my fingers around her amethyst pendant in my pocket and stroke it. I feel closer to her when I touch it, like a part of her is still mine. I found it in the meadow after I turned back Time. She must have lost it during our divine moments of passion. I didn't get the chance to return it to her because she was whipped away by Apollo. And Roman leaving with them, well that almost caused me to freeze time then and there. But I stood strong, held my nerve. I won't let that situation hinder my plans. She belongs to me.

I am waiting Siriarna and when the time is right, we will once again be together. I know it is our destiny.

******

Siriarna

I *am* a god. 'Goddess of Above' to be exact. The title bestowed upon me by my father in the Council Arena, the Olympian Gods bearing witness.

I am home. Home in a realm I didn't know I belonged. But I do. Belong that is. Warmth spreads throughout my body. An internal glow fills my soul, my aura reaching up to my crown. In my mind's eye I see the faint outline of a halo perched above my head. I look to Apollo, my eyes now level with his. His expression is one of expectancy. He knew. All along, he has known.

I see Psyche gasp as my transformation is completed. Her mouth is spread into a forced smile and her face is hardened, almost frozen into a faux cheerfulness. On the contrary, Zeus' face is the picture of delight.

For some strange reason, at this very moment, my thoughts return to Braxton and my heart skips a beat. I don't understand the sensation, it's almost like a reverse déjà vu.

One thing I am absolutely certain of is that I have access to a great power. And I know exactly what I need to do.

******

Contact Prudence Willett

Instagram | TikTok | Facebook : @prudencewillettwrites

Website: prudencewillett.com

Leave a Review

If you loved Siriarna, please consider leaving a positive review. Word of mouth is also a great way to introduce your friends to the Divine Destinies Trilogy.

The trilogy continues with Book 2, Alexandraya; where Vengeance, vows and vehemency await!

ABOUT THE AUTHOR

Prudence worked in the entertainment industry for 15 years. Her passion has always been in the written word.

She loves the escapism of reading, and creating her own fantasy world, was a labour of love.

Having lived in the city and the desert, she now resides by the sea with her husband and two children. Her writing buddy, Prince Whiskey, the enormous ragdoll cat, is always by her side offering many purrfect sounds of encouragement.

Prudence has a wicked sense of humour, a quirky personality, and loves nothing more than a lengthy chat.

ACKNOWLEDGEMENTS

To my mum, Judy Eckford, for uncovering a passion laid dormant. And for enduring endless conversations about this book. Thank you Mumsie, you're the best!

To my sister, Abigail Jane, for many late night power editing chat sessions and for being the best Sista Friend a girl could ask for.

To my daughter, Trixie Lee, for her honest feedback, clever edits, and endless encouragement.

To my son, Lawson, for his belief in me, and his exquisite map creation.

To my husband, Tasman, for his unwavering support.

And to Lascelles Morgan III, for his investment in the story, and his true friendship. Come along, come along...

<u>PLAY LIST</u>

- ❖ The Humming – Enya
- ❖ Following the Sun – Super-Hi x Neeka
- ❖ Wildest Dreams – Taylor Swift
- ❖ Firefly – Owl City
- ❖ Wake Me Up – Avici
- ❖ Reckless – Australian Crawl
- ❖ Rolling in the Deep – Adele
- ❖ Royal – Lorde
- ❖ Creepin–Metro Boomin, The Weeknd & 21 Savage
- ❖ Sound of Silence – Disturbed
- ❖ Worst Day of My Life – Amy Shark
- ❖ Fight Song – Rachel Platten
- ❖ Hello – Adele
- ❖ 10:35 – Tiesto & Tate McRae
- ❖ Lover – Taylor Swift
- ❖ Until I Found You – Stephen Chanchez/Em Beihold
- ❖ Perfect Duet – Ed Sheeran (with Beyoncé)
- ❖ Miss You – Oliver Tree & Robin Schultz
- ❖ In My Blood – Shawn Mendes
- ❖ Wrecking Ball – Miley Cyrus
- ❖ Beggin – Maneskin
- ❖ Silence (Feat. Sarah McLaclan) – Delerium
- ❖ Mercy –Duffy
- ❖ True Colours – Cindi Lauper

www.ingramcontent.com/pod-product-compliance
Lightning Source LLC
Chambersburg PA
CBHW010259100726
47904CB00011B/2664